HAZE

HAZE

a novel

New York Times Bestselling Author
Deborah Bladon

FIRST ORIGINAL KINDLE EDITION,
DECEMBER 2015

ISBN-13: 978-1519725769
ISBN-10: 1519725760
eBook ISBN: 978-1-926440-33-0

Book & cover design by Wolf & Eagle Media
Image by Alan Shapiro

www.deborahbladon.com

Also by Deborah Bladon

THE OBSESSED SERIES
THE EXPOSED SERIES
THE PULSE SERIES
THE VAIN SERIES
THE RUIN SERIES
IMPULSE
SOLO
THE GONE SERIES
FUSE
THE TRACE SERIES
CHANCE
THE EMBER SERIES
THE RISE SERIES

ACKNOWLEDGMENTS

When I'm writing or releasing a book, it's more than just me. I am thankful to have an incredible support system lifting and guiding me to the finish line, each and every single time. Here are a few of those amazing people:

Thank you to my family, for the long nights, the busy days, knowing when I need a break and always ensuring I had a sugary concoction from Starbucks in my hands. You are all my whole life and thank you for supporting my dream.

Thank you to M, for having more faith in me than I had in myself.

Thank you to A.J. for helping me to close my eyes to make a wish. It came true.

Thank you to my Amazon team, I rely on you more than you know.

And the biggest thank you to the readers. *The Bladon Babes*. Without you, none of this is possible. It has been the utmost pleasure writing stories for you and if you're reading this, thank you for investing in me one more time.

CHAPTER ONE

Isla

"How long have you worked here?" His voice is cultured, deep and smooth. It's not uncommon to hear a voice like that in this boutique. I've worked here for six weeks now and at least twice a week a man with too much money and an insatiable need to see young women dressed in expensive lingerie will come waltzing through the doors.

"Welcome to Liore," I say softly as I glance to my left to where he's standing.

I have to look up. He's large, not just in height but in his shoulder's breadth. His eyes are a rich brown, his hair just as dark. His nose is sculptured and his strong jaw only adds to his exceptionally striking features. The suit he's wearing is dark blue, perhaps even black. It's hard to tell under the chandelier lights that decorate this opulent space.

"Isla." His eyes hover over my chest before they settle on my name tag. "It's nice to meet you, Isla."

"It's lovely to meet you…" I pause. It's not only because I've been instructed to grab the name of each customer to give them a personal shopping experience. I want to know his name.

"Gabriel," he offers with a light touch of his hand on mine.

The name is oddly familiar. As I work to place it, I see him peering across the boutique at my boss.

1

"Is there something I can help you find, Gabriel? Are you purchasing something for a girlfriend, or perhaps, your wife?"

His expression shifts slightly. "I have neither."

That's a pity but it's not. This is exactly the type of man I envisioned in my mind's eye when I arrived in Manhattan. I graduated from high school less than two years ago and my dreams of attending Juilliard on a scholarship had vanished as quickly as my clean record when I broke one too many rules in high school.

"Is there something in particular that you're looking for?" I catch the faint wave of the hand of one of my co-workers across the aisle. I ignore it because when a customer is ready to buy, the store could be engulfed in flames, and I'm not moving an inch. The commissions here are the highest I've ever earned in retail and the secret to guarantee a big sale is to make the customer feel as though they're the only one in the boutique.

His eyes scan the various bras we have displayed before they move to the lace panties and garters. "If I asked you to try something on for me, Isla, would you do that? Would you take me into one of the change rooms with you?"

I've read the employee handbook. No, I skimmed it briefly while on my way to work that first day weeks ago. The number one rule is to never take a male customer into the rooms. Men who lead you into those quiet spaces are craving more than a private fashion show. I know that. "I'm sorry, Gabriel. That's against company policy."

He studies my face carefully. The dark shadow around my blue eyes looks hideous in the alarming bright light of the morning, but in here it's sensual and alluring. My shoulder length blonde hair is straight today, a sharp contrast to my high cheekbones. I'm here to sell lingerie and the light pink wrap around dress I'm wearing accentuates everything it needs to. He hasn't walked away yet, so he's still primed to buy.

He closes the short distance between us as he steps towards me. "You don't strike me as the type of young woman who follows all the rules."

It's tempting. Not just because of the extra money I'd find in my pocket. "I don't follow rules, Gabriel. If you want a private show, I can come to your office after work."

His brow cocks with the suggestion. "Is that something you offer to customers often?"

I've never offered it before. "I only offer it to the ones who peak my interest."

"I'll give you my card." His hand dips into the inner pocket of his suit jacket.

I take it from his long, elegant fingers and look down at it. I don't have time to read the details before my boss, Cicely, is upon us.

I turn to look at her but she's staring at Gabriel. Her hand leaps to his shoulder.

"Mr. Foster," she says slowly. "I see that you've met our newest girl. Isla, you're explaining everything we offer to Mr. Foster, yes?"

I look down at the card of Mr. Gabriel Foster, the CEO of Foster Enterprises and the man who owns this boutique.

"Isla has been very cordial." He glides the tip of his index finger along my wrist. "She's coming by my office today. I'll expect you at four, Isla."

"At four," I repeat back. "I'll be there at four, sir."

His eyes skim slowly over my body before they stop on my face. "Don't be late and bring those samples we spoke of."

I freeze as his hand runs up my arm before he brushes past me towards the front of the shop.

***

"You didn't answer my question earlier." Cicely throws me an agitated look as she walks into the stockroom, her long dark curls bouncing against her back with each step she takes. "I need you to explain exactly what's going on."

I need her to back off.

Once Gabriel Foster left, my boss had turned her attention solely to me. She can't be more than twenty-eight-years-old, but her strict, no-nonsense approach to managing the store ages her considerably. She scolded me like a child when I was precisely four minutes late to a shift last week and she's constantly schooling me on how to upsell every customer.

I don't need her condescending attitude. I do my job well. I proved that in spades just ten minutes ago when my last customer left here with over eighteen hundred dollars of merchandise tucked into a signature pale peach shopping bag with the Liore logo emblazoned across it. Considering the fact that she came in looking for one pair of black panties, I'd call that a huge success.

"What question is that?" I ask without looking up from the cardboard box I'm currently unpacking.

Today is delivery day at the boutique which means every sales associate on duty has to put in an hour in the back sorting through the new merchandise to ready it before it can be displayed on the sales floor. I hate this part of my job because it means commissions that should be mine are instead being pocketed by one of my co-workers.

"The question about what is going on between you and Mr. Foster." She reaches into the box to yank out a short, yellow, satin robe. "You need to steam these before you hang them up."

I glance over to where the upright steamer is resting. I'd plugged it into the electrical socket immediately after I opened the box and saw how wrinkled everything was. I know how important impeccable presentation is to the Liore brand. "I'll take care of that, Cicely."

"Answer my question. What was Mr. Foster talking about? Why are you going to his office with samples?"

I make a frustrated noise under my breath. Confessing to her that I propositioned the owner of the company we both work for will cut my shift short, and it will essentially mean the end of my job. Cicely is definitely a *'by the book'* type. It's just one of the many ways we are polar opposites. I take a step towards the steamer with a robe in my hand, hoping she'll jump off her current train of thought and launch into a long-winded tutorial about how to use it properly, even though she's already demonstrated that to me a handful of times since I started working here.

"It's about the shipment of lace garter slips that arrived last week, isn't it?" The robe in her hand drops back into the box as she lets it fall from her grasp. "That must be why he was here today. I was personally supposed to verify the quality of that order and report back to him. It completely slipped my mind."

I half-shrug my shoulder as I watch her scurry across the floor to an unopened box. This is the most flustered I've seen her and I have to admit, it's a good look for her.

"Drop all of that." Her hands both wave in the air in my direction. "We need to get these ready so we can take them to his office at four o'clock."

"We?" I cling tightly to the robe in my fist. "I think Mr. Foster just wanted to see me. He didn't say anything about you."

Any semblance of vulnerability leaves her expression as her perfectly tweezed dark brows rise. "Have you forgotten that you work for me, Isla Lane? You don't know the first thing about these samples. They're one of the new products that Mr. Foster just approved. I'll go with you. You'll watch and learn."

I don't say another word as I toss the robe I'm holding back into the box and walk across the room towards her. As frustrating as Cicely is and as much as I detest having her breathing over my shoulder on a daily basis, having her in this meeting may be my saving grace. I just might be able to salvage my job, if I play my cards right.

CHAPTER TWO

Gabriel

I see my mother through the open doors of my office before she turns to look at me. In that instant, I'm reminded that I arranged this meeting. I ordered her here because I need answers.

As I watch her make small talk with my assistant, I can't help but admire how she carries herself around others. She appears confident to a fault. The way she holds her shoulders back is evidence of that. You'd never know by looking at her that she's as careless and reckless as she is. She knows that there's little I can do to remedy her behavior other than to explain the impact her actions have on the business, as a whole. There's no doubt in my mind that she recognizes the risk she's taking. It's what energizes her and pushes her forward.

I reach to tap on the frame of the wooden double doors but it's unnecessary. Her dark eyes catch mine as her gaze wanders the reception area. She's bored with whatever, Sophia, my assistant is talking about. That's clear to me. Sophia, on the other hand, is oblivious to her disinterest and only ups the volume of her voice. The clattered chatter of her words is filling the space, seeping into my office.

"Gabriel." An instant smile courses over my mother's deep red lips. "I'm early."

She's not.

I'd asked her to meet me almost an hour ago. She'd countered with a proposed dinner meeting, but my plans for tonight are non-negotiable. When I'd explained that I needed her in my office no later than three, she'd told me she'd make it by five. It's a quarter to four now.

"Join me in my office." I hold her gaze, waiting for her to dismiss Sophia with a thoughtless flick of her wrist. It's the same gesture she's used on me time and again.

"Your secretary is telling me the most outlandish tale about a bullfrog."

My eyes drop to the marble floor in an attempt to mask the grin that I feel on my lips. "A bullfrog?"

"She asked where I grew up, Mr. Foster," Sophia goes on, "I was telling her about some of the things I saw back home."

I look up and directly at her. I have no idea where '*home*' is to her. She was a quick hire after my last assistant quit on the spot more than three months ago. Her name escapes me but the vile loathing in her eyes when I refused her request for an extra week's vacation to accommodate her honeymoon was memorable.

All the pent up resentment she'd held within for the eighteen months she worked for me had collided with her better judgment and had won. She'd hurled a barrage of insults at me in such rapid succession that I struggled to distinguish one from the other.

Once her peace was said, I calmly informed her that the two weeks of vacation time she'd previously requested had been approved months earlier and tacking on *'a few more days'* as she casually put it, would eat into my time in London during fashion week. I needed her there with me, not on a beach in the Caribbean drinking cocktails crafted from tropical fruit and flavored rum.

"We need to talk, mother," I say, ignoring the expected question about Sophia's childhood and the amphibian that apparently played an important role in the story of her life. "You can continue this conversation when we're done."

She shoots me a look that carries a veiled warning of something intended to be menacing. It may have worked, and likely did, when I was still a child, but now that I'm thirty-two-years old and running an international conglomerate that boasts our shared surname, the impact it has is fleeting, at best.

"You're asking me to be rude, Gabriel." She yanks softly on the diamond earring that is hanging from her left ear. "I'm just getting to know Sophia. You can wait a few minutes while we finish up."

It's now clear that she knows exactly why I insisted she make time for me today. It's also obvious why she lobbied for a discussion over dinner. She wanted the security that a crowded restaurant would bring. My mother knows me well enough to recognize that discussing family business in public isn't something I willfully do. That has a time and place, and regardless of what my mother wants, the time is right now.

"This can't wait." I motion towards my office. "We need to talk. That needs to happen now."

Her lips etch into a firm, thin line as she tosses her purse and coat on Sophia's desk in an overly dramatic gesture before she walks straight towards me.

***

"Your father would have no part of this." She arches her neck to once again look at the now closed doors of my office. It's the third time she's done it since I suggested she sit on the black leather sofa before I sat next to her. "He wouldn't approve of this at all."

I unbutton my suit jacket. "When is the last time you spoke to him?"

"Why? It doesn't matter when I spoke to him."

It actually does.

Since their divorce more than a decade ago my parents' broken relationship has swung on a pendulum from adoration to unconstrained contempt, bordering on hatred. The latter usually is in play when my father brings his latest companion to a company function in full view of my mother.

The string of dalliances he's had since they separated has been with women younger than me who view him as a tolerable rung on the ladder to success. Not one of the dozen or so women who have flirted their way into my father's life has lasted more than a few months.

"You know how much I value your input, Mother." I lean back wanting my body language to convey my message just as much as my words. I've learned in the most difficult way possible, through much trial and error, that the only way to handle Gianna Foster effectively is to make her feel valued and irreplaceable. "You also know that I'm not hiring any new designers at the moment."

She scratches the top of her forehead. The motion pushes a few strands of her deep brown hair aside. My mother has never made a secret of her pursuit of youth. She's on a first name basis with at least three of the most prestigious plastic surgeons in Manhattan. In her ongoing effort to recapture the face that once was reflected back in the mirror, she's lost the natural glow she had when I was a child. I remember back then thinking that she was the most beautiful woman I'd ever seen. Now, as I look at her perfect complexion, I see a woman battered within by the ever moving hands of time.

"Did your father put you up to this? Is that what this is about?"

It's an underhanded tactic devised to halt the conversation in its tracks. In the tug-of-war that was, and still is, the dissolution of their marriage, my parents viewed my two brothers and me as the ultimate prize. When we refused to take sides, my mother upped her game. Now, whenever there is a business related matter, she reverts back to blaming my father. He's too busy with his latest twenty-something girlfriend to even realize the company still exists.

"This is about Dante Castro." I stop for a beat before I continue, carefully considering my words. "He's a talented designer, but we have no place for him. You need to rescind the offer you made him."

Her jaw tightens at my words. "I'll do nothing of the sort. I already called a friend or two to announce that he's heading the men's division."

11

At last count, she'd called contacts at four of the premier fashion magazines. Each had reached out to me within the past two hours for my reaction to the announcement that my mother had secured the virtually unknown talents of a designer whose ability is questionable but whose presence is meant to make my father jealous. I'm not about to hand over the reins of our men's fashion line to someone whose claim to fame is designing t-shirts emblazoned with logos for skateboarding aficionados.

"You need to call him now." I tap the fingers of my left hand on her knee. "He's not a good fit for us."

"He's a perfect fit." Her bottom lip juts out in a pout. "Gabriel, I've already made the announcement. How would it look if I didn't give him the job?"

I push out a quick puff of air from between my lips, tempted to tell her that the position is already filled by one of the most creative designers in the world today. That would fall on her deaf, and now frustrated, ears. "If you can't handle it, Mother, I can. Give me the word and I'll make this disappear before the official announcement sees the light of day."

"Do it," she says as she smooths her hands over the fabric of her navy blue slacks. "Fix it the way you always do."

CHAPTER THREE

Isla

I nervously fumble with my smartphone as I sit in the reception area at Foster Enterprises. Cicely had stuck to her plan for us to bring each and every lace garter slip that was packed in the box she ripped open, to Mr. Foster's office with us.

We'd shoved the overstuffed Liore bags into the trunk of a taxi outside the store. I briefly argued the point that the tennis shoes that were already occupying the cramped space smelled like a dead body, but Cicely was too amped up on adrenaline to even acknowledge that I was along for the ride.

We've sat here for almost thirty minutes now and Cicely has used at least twenty-nine of those to quietly rehearse what sounds like a late night infomercial about the undeniable alluring qualities of the over-priced garter slips we brought along with us.

If she'd bothered to ask my opinion, which she hasn't, I would have told her to bring one and that if honesty is what Mr. Foster wants, a critique about the quality of the materials and the location of the hooks for fastening would be first on my list.

"Do you like working at the boutique?"

My gaze jumps from the addictive game I'm playing on my smartphone to the face of the woman who greeted us when we stepped off the elevator and approached Mr. Foster's office. The space is large and airy. The furnishings are exquisite and the walls are painted light grey.

The only spot of brightness is the woman behind the desk, Sophia. She has a slight southern drawl that reminds me of my third grade teacher. She's pretty, but in a muted, unassuming, way.

I glance towards Cicely who is still in full-on preparation mode. I will the doors of Mr. Foster's office to open but they don't. Engaging in idle talk about a job I may no longer have, isn't helping with my increasing anxiety. If I'm fired, I want to know so I can start looking for something else to fill in my time until my future really begins.

"It's a wonderful place to work," I try to sound as sincere as I can. "Do you like working here?"

There's a slight pause as her eyes flit across the room towards the closed doors. I see the hesitation in her expression before I hear it in her words. "I'm very lucky that I have this position."

I should push and ask for more but the details of why there's a hint of disgruntled dissatisfaction in her tone doesn't matter to me. I'll likely be off the Foster Enterprises payroll within the hour and I'll never set eyes on her again.

I clear my throat with the intention of saying something trivial about the weather and the cool breeze that took over the city this afternoon but I'm stalled when the doors to Mr. Foster's office burst open.

Cicely and I turn in unison to see a beautiful woman dressed in dark pants and a white blouse walk through the double doors towards us. As she turns back briefly, her rich brown hair brushes her shoulders.

From where I'm sitting, I can't see the person she reaches for but I know it has to be him. It takes just a few seconds for her to confirm that in a hushed tone. "You've always been my favorite, Gabriel. You will always be my favorite."

A deep chuckle fills the room as he steps forward, into view, to scoop her hand into his. As he raises it to his lips, he looks down into her face. "Asher is your favorite, Mother. We all know that he is."

She shakes her head briefly before she reaches up to touch her lips to his cheek.

"Mr. Foster." Cicely ignores any sense of decency and interrupts the tender moment by jumping to her feet. Her hands run over the skirt of the simple brown dress she's wearing. "We were here early, sir. You said we should be here at four o'clock. We were here by three fifty. I just want you to know that."

With her words, his eyes leave his mom's face and dart to Cicely and then settle on me, lingering there until his mom taps his chest. "Do I want to know what this is about? What are these two doing with all those Liore shopping bags? Is this some kind of clothing drive? Do they work at a shelter?"

I push back the urge to laugh at the suggestion that we're collecting expensive lingerie to clothe the city's least fortunate. As much as the comment amuses me, it maddens Cicely. "I'm the manager of the Liore boutique, Ma'am. You're Gianna Foster, aren't you?"

The hand that Cicely extends hangs in the air for several seconds before Gianna tentatively grabs hold of it with her own. "I'm Gianna Foster. What are you doing here? If you manage the store, you should be there, no?"

Yes, Mrs. Foster, she should. Instead, she's on a crusade to defend ugly ass garter slips and I'm along for the ride.

"I come bearing samples of one of our new items." She swings both her arms so wildly in the air that she stumbles backwards, her heel tapping the edge of one of the bags causing it to fall over spilling most of its contents on the polished floor.

Gianna grimaces as she drops Cicely's hand to point towards the garter slips that are now in full view. "Look what you've done."

Before Cicely has a chance to turn to pick up the slips, I'm on my knees, pushing them back into the bag. I would have been happy to stay where I was but if I'm going to hold onto this job, I need to make at least one good impression on Gabriel Foster. This may be my only chance.

The room falls silent except for the sound of shoes against the marble floor. I catch a glimpse of a black wingtip oxford just as it comes into view. There's little time for me to react before I sense him crouching next to me. I suck in a deep breath hoping that he won't fire me in front of all these women while I'm on all fours with a handful of lingerie.

"Allow me to help." His breath races across my cheek as he leans in to scoop up the lingering pieces.

16

I only nod softly in agreement as my breath catches when his hand brushes against mine. The touch, matched with the scent of his exquisite cologne, and the sound of his voice, makes me feel momentarily light-headed. I close my eyes hoping to ward off the sensation and the temptation to lean against him.

"You have your hands full, son." Gianna's voice pulls Gabriel back to his feet. "I'm leaving. I'll call you tomorrow."

"Tomorrow," he repeats. "I'll take care of that issue we discussed before the end of the day."

Just as I stand I catch Gianna, with her coat and purse in hand, rounding the corner towards the elevator.

"Mr. Foster." Cicely stands in front of Gabriel. "I'm prepared to go over the samples with you."

"Samples?" His hands jump to the silver necktie he's wearing. He straightens it, keeping his eyes trained on my face. "These are the samples that were delivered last week?"

"These are the ones." She scoops two of the bags into her hands as she brushes past him on her way into his office.

I follow her lead because right now, Cicely owns this meeting with her misplaced sense of why we are even in the Foster Enterprises building. Mr. Foster doesn't seem fazed that we arrived together with this much of his product in hand. Maybe I did misjudge what happened back at the boutique.

I pick up the remaining two bags and take a step towards his office. Any relief I may have felt is wiped away in a single second as I feel his hand catch hold of my elbow. His breath races over my cheek when he leans down and close, his voice low enough that only I can make out the words. "I wanted you here alone, Isla. I thought I made that clear."

Fuck. Just, fuck.

I don't turn to look at him when I feel his hand drop away. I pull in a deep breath, walk into his office and wait for his next move.

CHAPTER FOUR

Gabriel

"I apologize for the delay," I say as I close my office doors behind me. "A matter came up that couldn't be ignored."

Cicely, the boutique manager, nods vigorously in understanding even though it's now near five o'clock. After my mother left, I'd retreated to one of the empty boardrooms to make the inevitable call changing the course of Dante Castro's career. I half-expected more push on his end but he'd taken the news with calm resignation.

I anticipated at least a question or two about why the offer was being pulled but there was none of that. His voice had lowered as he told me he understood and with that the call ended.

I'd spent the next thirty minutes connecting with the magazine contacts to correct what I called, *'a simple oversight on the part of one of our internal managers.'*

I see no need to embarrass my mother. If I can't find a workaround to save her from humiliation, I'll craft one. It's all part of helming both the business, and my family. It certainly helped when I offered each contact backstage access to our showing during fashion week here in New York.

"Should I begin now?" Cicely springs from her chair. "I arranged the garter slips on the sofa by color."

I look toward the large black sofa that I sat on not more than an hour ago with my mother. Draped over the back cushions and armrests are pieces of lingerie.

"I prepared a presentation." Cicely glances down at her smartphone. "I have my notes open. I'm ready whenever you are, sir."

Unlike Cicely, Isla is sitting quietly, her legs crossed at the knee as her right foot bobs up and down. Her hands are resting in her lap, discreetly holding the front of the skirt of her pink dress in place.

When I'd entered the room, Cicely's head was the only one that turned. Isla's shoulders had tensed briefly before they relaxed once her manager spoke.

I made no mention of Cicely coming to my office when I was at the boutique earlier. I'm not sure what Isla did to convince her boss to tag along but it's impressive. I admire creativity and tenacity. It changes absolutely nothing though.

Isla's proposition was all I needed to extend the invitation. Regardless of who is doing the offering, sexual favors for customers is grounds for dismissal. She may be a new hire but there's no room for excuse. Any employee who doesn't follow company guidelines is expendable; even if that person has a face that can stop traffic and a body that can bring a man to his knees.

She caught me off guard when I walked into the boutique earlier today. I'd noticed her well before I approached her. I'd stood just inside the door watching her move as she rearranged a display. My intention to speak with Cicely had disappeared the moment I saw Isla.

She'd readjusted each piece of lingerie, her hands delicate as they took care to line the panties on the table symmetrically. Every few seconds, she'd raise her head to scan the area near where she stood. I recognized that as a natural desire to find her next customer. She was primed to hunt. Even though she appeared busy with her task at hand, her goal wasn't to present our product in the best light she could, it was to make another sale.

My body reacted when she'd turned to the side and I caught my first glimpse of her profile. The generous curves of her body beneath the dress were inviting. She's breathtaking, petite, and, I imagine, incredible to fuck. She's also at least a decade younger than me.

When she looked into my eyes and offered to come to my office, my cock stiffened. I was hard as nails until Cicely touched my shoulder and reminded me where I was.

Business is business and pleasure has no place there. I keep them separated out of need. I've never touched a woman who works for me. It would breed a sort of complication I don't have the time or the inclination to deal with.

"I'm impressed with the samples, Mr. Foster," Cicely begins what I know, from experience, will be a long winded accounting of every aspect of what looks like the lace and mesh garter slips I had her order several weeks ago. The woman is good at her job but she's wound too tight. "I can go over the highlights for you now."

Or you can get the hell out so I can take Isla over my knee.

I shake my head chasing the thought away while I keep my eyes honed in on Cicely. "In your opinion are they on par with the rest of Liore's offerings?"

"Oh, absolutely, sir," she chirps happily. "I think our customers are going to love them."

"I disagree," Isla interjects softly. "I don't like them at all."

I feel a smile tug at the corner of my mouth but I halt it as I turn to face her. "You disagree?"

A small sigh escapes as her tongue flies over her bottom lip, moistening it. "I wouldn't wear one."

Immediately I'm assaulted with the mental image of her body covered in nothing but a sheer slip. I push it aside knowing that within hours I'll likely be buried so deep within a woman I'll meet at the club tonight, that Isla will never cross my mind again. I can easily chase away the desire I'm feeling. I've done it with others when I've felt a pull I knew I'd have to resist.

"Isla," Cicely's voice breaks into the fray. "You can't say that."

"I'm not going to bullshit him," she spits back. "Those slips don't deserve space in the boutique. Did you even bother to look at them closely?"

"Mr. Foster, don't mind her. Isla is new." Cicely walks past me towards the sofa. "She's young. She's only twenty. She doesn't understand the business the way we do."

It's been said that you can't judge a book by its cover. For the most part, I believe the words hold value in many cases, but not all. As Isla rises from the chair, I'm captivated by the subtle sway of her hips as she walks across the room to follow Cicely.

She moves with a grace that most women, even those double or triple her age, never possess. She's sensual, composed, and within the focused glare of her stormy blue eyes is clear determination.

"What are you wearing under your dress?" She stops mere inches behind Cicely, her hands darting to her hips.

I move closer, intrigued by the challenge in her tone. Cicely whips around on her heel, her arms jumping to cross over her chest. She's at least four inches taller than Isla but their body language leaves little doubt about who is the prey. "Why would you ask me something like that? It's none of your business."

I'm standing next to them now, soaking in the view of them both. Isla is self-assured and calm, raking her eyes over Cicely's plain frame. Her lips part slightly before she tilts her head to the left, eyeing her manager's strappy heels. "You're not wearing Liore lingerie, are you?"

Cicely's hands impulsively jump to the waist of her dress, tugging on the thin brown leather belt. "You're out of line, Isla. My underwear isn't relevant."

"Is it Liore or not?" Isla moves her foot slightly, which reveals a glimpse of her toned, tanned leg.

"I'm not answering that." Cicely's gaze falls to the floor. "I don't have to answer that."

"You just answered it," Isla says softly before she moves to walk around Cicely. "I knew it when I first met you."

"Knew what? You don't know anything about me."

"You're wrong." Isla picks up one of the garter slips, holding it in the air between them. "I know that you buy your panties at a department store. I'd guess they're white cotton. You get them in a package of three or four and while you're there you take a bra off the rack without trying it on. You're a 32B, aren't you?"

Cicely's hand grazes across her chest. "Yes, but…"

"How can you judge these if you've never worn one?" Isla holds the slip in front of her. "The lace is brittle and rough. It's going to scratch."

I tuck my hands into the front pockets of my pants, intrigued by the exchange taking place right in front of me. I know I should step in and save Cicely from the lesson in lingerie but I'm too immersed in watching Isla to interfere.

"The fasteners are awkward and hard to reach." Isla flips the garment over. "You'd have to ask someone to help you put it on. That defeats the purpose."

"What purpose?" Cicely asks with what sounds like innocent ease.

Isla dips her chin as a sly smile flows over her lips. "A lot of our customer base comes in to the boutique to buy something for a special occasion."

Cicely shrugs her shoulder. "I don't get it."

"When I put on something like this," Isla begins as holds the garter slip against the front of her dress. "The last time I put on something like this, I did it myself so the first time my boyfriend saw it was at the end of our date, at the exact moment I wanted him to."

Boyfriend.

The word catches my breath in my throat as a tight knot forms in my gut. Naturally she'd have a boyfriend. Any man with a brain in his head would claim her for his own the first chance he had. It's more than likely some college kid with a perpetual hard-on, who doesn't give a shit about anything other than blowing his own load. Whoever he is, I doubt like hell he is giving her everything she needs or wants. If he was, she wouldn't have offered to come to my office this afternoon.

Jesus. What am I doing to myself? She works for me. She has a fucking boyfriend.

"You know that you're entitled to three hundred dollars of free lingerie a month, right?" Isla pushes the slip into Cicely's hands. "You should be wearing the products if you're selling them."

"We're not allowed to just take merchandise off the shelf." Cicely sighs. "Isla have you been taking things? Are you wearing Liore lingerie now?"

"I'm wearing a push up bra. It's that one from the Charming collection, in nude lace, and I have on the matching V-string panty."

I turn in an effort to hide my body's response to that. I feel a rush of heat race through me when my pulse quickens. My cock is aching, literally aching, inside the restraint of my pants.

I've headed this division for months now. I've seen some of the world's most beautiful women in the lingerie brand that I helped launch and yet, I've never had a reaction like this. It's visceral, intense and wholly unwelcome in this moment.

"It's in the employee handbook," Isla says quietly. "I asked Wallis when I started at the boutique and she showed me the paperwork that I have to fill out each month."

It's just another reason why I asked Wallis Clarkson to take the reins at the boutique. I'd brought her up from another division to oversee the opening of the store. She was insistent that Cicely was perfect for the manager position. It's why she stepped in as a consultant temporarily. Cicely's strength is in keeping the store organized, beyond that I'm seriously beginning to doubt how much value she's bringing.

"She's correct, Cicely," I interrupt, needing this meeting to end soon. In fact, now would not be fast enough. "Part of your benefit package is free merchandise. You should be taking advantage of that."

Her eyes dash from Isla's face back to mine. "I'll do that, sir. I'll start wearing Liore lingerie every day."

CHAPTER FIVE

Isla

At least I converted Cicely into a lingerie wearing, not-so-hot, Liore employee today. If I had the patience, and any interest at all, I'd also suggest that she stop raiding her grandmother's closet when she's getting dressed for work each day.

Who am I to judge? She's obviously going to walk out of here with a job and I'm going to be headed straight for…well, to my apartment most likely. I'm too exhausted to even think about looking for a new job tonight.

I tried to make a lasting impression with my knowledge of Cicely's underwear. She may believe that I can tell that she wears plain white panties and bras because it's obvious in the way she carries herself.

Truth be told, I caught a glimpse of her in the staff room after work one day trading out the hideous yellow pants and matching blouse she had on for her work out clothes. That's when I saw that she wasn't wearing anything sold at the boutique. It's actually an image that will be burned into the farthest back reaches of my mind forever.

"Isla is right." Mr. Foster rubs his fingers over the lace of one of the garter slips. "This isn't what I expected at all. I didn't approve this."

Cicely steps into place right next to him, her hands greedily reaching down to scoop up a black slip. "I have to agree. Our customers wouldn't find them acceptable at all."

For fuck's sake, Cicely. Really? Now, you agree with me?

"Pack them up and ship them back." He tosses the slip onto the sofa. "I'll make the necessary calls tomorrow and have a new sample sent with the materials I approved."

"I can bring that to your office as soon as it arrives," Cicely mutters under her breath as she pushes the garter slips back into the bags.

"No." He leans against the corner of his desk. "That's not necessary. I'll have it delivered here. Your attention should be on the boutique and the staff."

"Of course," she says while she nods her head. "I'm in charge there, after all."

I roll my eyes not caring if Gabriel Foster catches the movement or not. I doubt like hell that I've saved my job. I don't take an ounce of comfort in the fact that he hasn't brought up what happened in the store earlier.

He's been bombarded with dealing with Cicely and her impromptu meeting since we arrived. I expect to be next on his agenda which means I'll not only have to face his wrath but I'll have to do that with Cicely as a witness. If that's not karma, I'm not sure what is.

"Is there anything else that you need?" He crosses his arms over his chest as he watches Cicely fumble with the bags. "I assume that we've covered everything you came here to address."

"Yes, thank you, but if I think of anything else I'll call you." She pushes two of the bags towards me with her foot. "Isla and I will go back to the store and pack these up. She can drop them at the courier's office on her way home."

I turn to look at her, realizing that if I do indeed walk out of here with a job, I'm going to have to do everything she says since she is technically in control of my every movement at Liore.

"Isla won't be accompanying you back to the boutique." He takes a measured step towards us. "I need to have a word with her."

Cicely's brow furrows as she studies my face. "I'm her manager. Is it something I need to know about?"

"This doesn't concern you." His eyes are trained solely on my face. I know he's waiting for me to react but I won't. I'm not about to break in front of my manager. I don't want to give her a glimpse into that part of me. To her, I'm just another in a string of women, who will work at Liore for a short time before they mess up.

I've heard her sharing stories with Wallis while they've stocked shelves. I won't be the first, or the last, woman to be fired from the boutique by Mr. Foster. I just don't want to be the only who was fired by him in front of Cicely.

"Should I wait in the reception area?" She struggles to pick up all four of the shopping bags. "I can wait there until Isla is done."

"There's work for you to do at the boutique." He scoops the handle of two of the bags into his fists. "I'll have Sophia call a car for you. The driver will help with the bags."

She only nods faintly in response as he leads her towards the doors of his office and out of my view. As he closes the doors behind both of them, I slide back into the chair I was sitting in earlier to await my fate.

***

"If you're going to fire me, can you do that now?" I tap the toe of one of my nude heels against the polished marble floor. I haven't moved at all since he came back into the office and sat behind his desk. He'd been gone for close to twenty minutes, which felt longer than an eternity to me. "I don't like playing games."

My admission pulls a faint smile over his full lips. "You don't like playing games? Do I strike you as the type of man who engages in games, Isla?"

It's a loaded question. Judging by the fact that the building we're sitting in has his surname blazoned across the front of it, I'd guess that Gabriel Foster has played more than his fair share of corporate games to gain the upper hand in the cutthroat world of fashion. His company's designs are featured on the world's most prominent runways.

The Arilia line for women and the Berdine line for men set the tone for the company's success. The designs are classic and sophisticated.

I glanced at the price tag of two of the dresses from the spring collection when I tried them on a few weeks ago in a boutique in SoHo. I'd snapped selfies in the mirror before I slid them off my body and handed them back to the woman waiting outside the dressing room door. She'd sighed under her breath. It was a faint sound that carried the judgement of someone who thought I couldn't afford the expensive fabric that bore the Arilia brand.

I'd left the store and boarded a bus to take me to Liore for my shift. The Liore lingerie offering is new for the Foster brand but it's already selling well and for the time being, I'd like to keep myself attached to that in the form of a steady stream of commissions. That means I need to do damage control to convince Gabriel Foster that I don't normally plan secret, after work, meetings in the offices of the men who visit the store. I may have gained a few points when Cicely was in the room, but now it's just me fighting for my job.

"I don't think you play games," I try to sound genuine. "I didn't say that."

He leans forward, his dark eyes boring into me. "You offered me a private show in the comfort of my office. I'd like to understand exactly what that entails."

I nervously skim my hands over the thin fabric of the skirt of my dress. I glance down at my lap, the pale nude polish on my fingernails has chipped away leaving a jagged layer of shimmer that catches the light when I glide my hands towards my bare knees.

"Isla? Do you have an explanation for me?" he asks, his voice startling me.

I look up and across the desk to where he's sitting. It's the perch from where he runs his business and apparently also subtly intimates people. He's doing it to me now. I know he expects me to back down. Men like him always do. They think the fact that they have more life experience or a larger bank account means they can push me into a corner with their words, or in some cases, their bodies.

"It's not something I've done before," I admit. "I haven't made that offer to any other man who has come into the boutique."

His left brow arches as the corner of his lip rises. "I was your first?"

I keep my eyes trained on his face, watching the way his gaze slides over my lips before it falls to my neck. He's enjoying this. He's pulling some perverse pleasure from watching me squirm in this leather office chair.

He wants me to break and fall to my knees in apology so I can keep my job. I see it in the way his fingers are strumming the edge of his desk. He's relaxed and completely, utterly in control.

"You were the first." I dart my tongue over my bottom lip, suddenly feeling as though the air in his office is heavy and thick. "I shouldn't have offered to come to your office. I don't know why I did. I guess I wasn't thinking clearly."

He adjusts one silver cuff link, then the other, before he pushes himself gracefully to his feet. "Stand up, Isla."

I do it because I have no other choice, even though I'm not sure my knees won't buckle from the combination of stress and desire I'm feeling right now. I know logically that he's called me here to reprimand me for breaking one of the company's mandatory rules, but I can't help but wonder what he's like when he's not wearing the suit, and his focus is entirely on a woman he craves. He's different since he showed Cicely out. The energy he's exuding is rawer, more intense.

"In a case like this, company policy is clear," he says with no emotion.

The rasp in his voice resonates, pushing me back a step. I cross my arms over my chest. It's a restless gesture meant to help me gain my composure. My job is on the line here and even though I know I can score another retail gig tomorrow, I'll have to work twice as hard to make the money I'm pulling in at Liore. I just need this to tide me over until my birthday next month.

"I'm the best you'll ever have," I blurt out.

"You're the best I'll ever have?" His voice lowers as he steps towards me. "You'll need to explain that to me."

I sigh realizing how arrogant my words sound. "My sales are more than all the other girls combined. I work hard. I move merchandise. I'm an asset to Liore."

"I reviewed the numbers for last month this morning when I received them from accounting." He tips his chin towards his desk. "Your sales are impressive. I'm not going to argue that point."

I rub my fingertips over my forehead before I look up and into his face. "I made a stupid mistake earlier today, Mr. Foster. I guarantee that it will never happen again."

He glances down at the silver watch on his wrist. "This company is an extension of my family, Isla. I expect each and every employee of Foster Enterprises to follow the code of conduct that is outlined in the employee manual."

Yes, I know, and I broke it when I essentially offered to come to his office and give him a private lingerie show. "I don't have an excuse for my behavior, sir. I want this job. I like working at Liore. All I'm asking for is a second chance."

He tilts his head back just a touch as his eyes study mine. "You're still within the probationary period. One incident like this warrants termination."

My heart sinks at the words. It's not as though I'm planning a life of selling lingerie. I don't want that. I doubt that I'll willingly be working there three months from now. I need the money that the job affords me right now and the hours allow me to pursue the one thing I'm actually passionate about, my music.

Liore is in no way my be all and end all. It's a means to an end and for now, I don't want to give that up.

"Please consider my performance beyond what happened today." I look directly into his brown eyes certain that I feel something pass between us. "If you give me another chance, I promise that you won't regret it."

"I have no reassurance that this isn't something you do on a regular basis." His voice lowers. "You seemed very comfortable when you propositioned me."

I was very comfortable because it was exactly what I wanted. The magnetic pull I felt between us in the boutique has only heightened since I walked into his office. Who wouldn't proposition him? He's insanely gorgeous and hot as fuck.

"I thought you were attractive," I begin before I stop to pull in a deep breath. "You're obviously very attractive, sir. I just wanted to have some fun. I don't normally do things like that. I'm not like that."

"What are you like?" he asks, startling me with the question.

"What am I like?" I parrot back. "I'm not sure I know what you mean."

A small smile touches his lips. "From what I've witnessed today you're a very ambitious, hard-working woman who isn't afraid to go after what she wants. Beyond that my knowledge of you is limited to how astute you are regarding our products and the fact that you have a boyfriend."

"No." I exhale in a rush. "I don't have a boyfriend but you're right, I work very hard. I believe I work harder than anyone else in the store."

His brows lift. "No boyfriend? You mentioned him when you were speaking to Cicely about the garter slips."

Embarrassed, I shift on my feet, wishing he hadn't demanded that I stand. I feel off balance. "I was referring to my last boyfriend. We dated in Chicago before I moved here. He liked pretty lingerie."

"I see," he murmurs under his breath. "I misunderstood that. I didn't misunderstand the proposition though. It's difficult to overlook that."

"I realize that," I say, my voice sounding pitchy and breathy. "If I could take it back, I would. It was a mistake, sir. We all make them sometimes."

He turns his head slightly to break my gaze before he takes a step back. "I have to be somewhere this evening. If it wasn't for that, we'd continue this conversation but I need to end it here."

I feel a sense of panic welling up within me. It makes no sense. I should take my bruised pride and leave, never to look back, but I can't. I don't even want to think about going through another series of interviews, in an effort to try and impress a stranger just to get another dead end job. I just want to keep going to Liore and selling lingerie until I get my life sorted. "Mr. Foster, I won't let you down. I'll prove to you that I'm an asset. I won't do what I did today again. You have my word."

He turns, his hands jumping to fasten the top button on his tailored suit jacket. "Very well, Isla. We'll revisit this in a few days. I don't have time right now. You'll see yourself out."

"I can go back to work tomorrow?" My voice betrays me as I sound much more excited than I actually am.

"You'll remain an employee," he begins before he stops himself, his eyes riveted to my lips. "You are an employee, for now. That changes instantly if you cross another line."

I don't say a word. I give him a quick nod, pick up my purse and head straight for the doors.

CHAPTER SIX

Gabriel

"I missed you last night, Gabriel." Her voice is expectant and impatient. "I waited for you until well past midnight."

They're the words of a woman I'll never sleep with again.

I made that mistake, more than three years ago when we met at a club on the Lower East Side. I was alone, nursing a glass of scotch, when she sat next to me.

I was seeking solace there after arriving on the heels of a business deal gone south. I was angry, wanting and when her hand brushed against my thigh, I'd grabbed hold of it and pulled her into me. What began as a kiss between strangers ended with her in a broken heap on my office floor two months later.

I'd taken her to a room at an hourly rate hotel minutes after we met. It was small, disgusting, and afforded me everything I needed to drag her into the pit of desperation I was in at the time. I'd fucked her roughly, used her, and when it was done, she'd begged for it again.

I'd given in the next night and for countless nights after that, not because my body couldn't resist her. It was the escape that I craved.

Each night was a repeat of the one before with less emotion. Until finally one night with each drive of my cock down her throat I felt the emptiness grow.

When I looked down at her face covered in a mixture of sweat, her lipstick, and my release, I saw my own regret.

I'd ended it then; told her that it wasn't her but as the days wore on and her persistence grew, my patience waned. She called, sent hundreds of emails, and text messages and then the day she arrived at my office in nothing but a trench coat, I'd been as brutal as I'd ever been.

I was cold and callous as I told her that she was nothing to me. I'd ordered her out of my office, my life, and the city, if I recall. I wanted her gone and as I grabbed her hand to yank her towards the door, she'd collapsed. She'd fallen onto the floor, weeping and whispering words about love and connection.

I stood there, above her, resolute and unyielding as I pulled her back to her feet, closed the coat around her nude body and had security escort her to the street.

I avoided the club for more than two years after that. I chased my need to satisfy my desires when I traveled. I'd meet women in Rome or London and when the night was done, they were forgotten as easily as the movie I'd watch on the flight there.

Months ago, when I finally ventured back into that same club she sat next to me again when I ordered my drink. I flinched when she touched my leg. I pushed her hand back into her own lap and then I looked at her face and when I did I saw something much different.

She'd been married, divorced, and engaged again during the years we didn't speak. She was there with her fiancé, a high profile banker from Wall

Street who she met at a concert. I shook his hand, excused myself and realized that her desperate behavior years before had nothing to do with me after all. It was the drive within her to find someone to cherish her and she had.

"How's Clinton?" I ask only because if her fiancé is no longer in the picture, she has no place near me. "When's the wedding?"

"Your invitation is in the mail." She doesn't hesitate as she takes a seat next to me at the table. "Will you bring a plus one?"

If the intention of the question is anything more than the obvious, I'm not aware. We've come a long way and although I'd never include her in my circle of friends, she's no longer my enemy. There are parts of me that she's seen that I need to protect and the best way for me to do that now, is to be cordial. "Unfortunately, my schedule is full, Sage, but I'll send a gift. Where are you registered?"

She ignores the question in favor of ordering a drink when the waiter approaches. "Why weren't you at the club? I assumed you'd be there."

I push my lunch aside, my appetite suddenly vanishing. "Did my assistant tell you I'd be here?"

Her green eyes scan the posh interior of Axel NY before they settle back on me. "I dropped by your office to catch up. She told me you were doing some business over lunch but, alas, here you are alone."

I make a mental note to instruct Sophia on the finer points of dealing with Sage Butler which include never telling her where I am. "What do you want?"

Her gaze falls on the server who is now approaching with her lemon drop martini. "I need a sip before we talk."

I need an entire bottle of scotch before I can carry on a full blown conversation with Sage but I have three meetings that need my attention this afternoon. The glass I've half consumed is my limit for the day. I'll have to rely on that to get me through the remainder of my now ruined lunch.

She sips the drink carefully, rolling the liquid around on her tongue before she swallows it. She tilts her head back slightly. A man sitting at the table next to us watches her movements, his eyes focused on her short black hair. It's styled wildly which only further reflects the woman she can be. The rest of her is flawless, right down to her expensive heels and the impressive diamond ring adorning her left hand.

"What is it, Sage? You've got five minutes before I need to leave."

My words are met with a frown and yet another sip of the martini. "Why weren't you at the club? I wanted to talk to you. I met someone there I think you'll like."

I rub the back of my neck as I watch a server speaking to a couple standing near the entrance. Her hair is blonde and straight, skimming just below her jawline. She's rail thin, clumsy and from what I've seen, not good at her job.

I noticed her the moment I was seated. Her hair color caught my attention out of the corner of my eye. It's the same shade as Isla's but that's where the similarities end. The brief reminder of the woman who convinced me to give her a second chance has been my companion throughout my lunch.

Hell, she's been on my mind since she walked out of my office last night, leaving a trail of her fragrance in her wake. It was a simple combination of jasmine and her skin. It was light, airy and intoxicating.

I had essentially driven her out of the door to halt the temptation I felt to push her on what she was going to do when she invited herself to my office. I wanted to hear the words. I wanted her to tell me step-by-step what would have happened if I wasn't Gabriel Foster, the man who owns Liore, and then I wanted her to show me.

I'd poured myself a drink and sat in my chair after Sophia took her leave. I stared at the lights of lower Manhattan while visions consumed me of things that I'll never have.

Isla spread nude on the sofa in my office with my face buried between her thighs.

Isla in my bed, her perfectly round ass in the air as her greedy whimpers fill the still space.

I take what I want from the women I desire. Once I've had them it's easy to push them aside in favor of who is waiting around the corner. That works well for most women.

I know myself well enough to know when one taste won't be enough. It would be that way with Isla. I felt that the moment she turned to me at the boutique and looked up into my eyes. She has the power to wreck a man, to drive him to his knees in pathetic desperation.

I doubt she even realizes it yet. She's blissfully unaware of the impact she had on me.

It was after one in the morning when I finally called for my driver and left the office, heading home to the spacious, barren penthouse that I've worked so hard for. I'd taken a shower, not cold, but tepid. It did nothing to quell my desire. I knew I could stroke my cock until I came but that would only relieve the physical pressure. Nothing will quiet the suffocating need or want.

I don't know her.

I can't have her.

I need to forget her.

"Gabriel, you're not listening to me, are you?"

I rake my hand through my hair. "I'm not interested, Sage."

"I haven't even told you about her." She finishes her drink in one swift swallow, her tongue lashing out to scoop up any stray liquid off her lips. "She's perfect for you. I know what you like. It wouldn't hurt to meet her."

I chuckle as I open my wallet to retrieve a few bills. I toss them on the table as I stand, reaching down to bring the glass of scotch to my mouth. I drink it all. The liquid burns a hot path across my tongue and down my throat. "It wouldn't hurt me but we both know it would hurt her."

CHAPTER SEVEN

Isla

"You didn't leave a note, Isla." His voice startles me as I walk over the threshold and into my apartment. "I woke up and you were gone."

I stop in my tracks and stare at him. He's dressed in grey sweatpants and absolutely nothing else. His firm chest is on full display even though he knows he's not supposed to wander around half-clothed. She's nagged him for that time and time again. She may be my very best friend, but apparently she has little trust that I won't throw myself at her boyfriend full force.

"Nigel," I say his name quietly, hoping that I'll be able to find at least a t-shirt he can throw on before Cassia wakes up and discovers he's not in bed with her. "Put on some clothes."

"You said we'd talk about things this morning." He walks towards the sofa, taking long strides. I feel an immediate sense of relief when he tugs a blue sweater over his head. "I got up early so we could do that."

I scrub my hand over my face, pushing a few wayward strands of my hair back in place. "I went for a run. I needed to burn off some energy."

His eyes scan the hallway, stopping to focus on Cassia's bedroom door. "She's fast asleep. She worked late again last night."

I can't say I'm surprised. Cassia Moncton is the essence of focus and drive. We went to high school together in Chicago and as soon as we graduated, her life propelled itself into a completely different direction than mine.

She moved to Manhattan to attend Columbia on a full scholarship. She landed a spot as an intern at Hughes Enterprises in their software development division. Her life is on a track she's planned since before we even met.

The only thing missing is the husband she always talked about when we were younger. Nigel seems to think he can fit the bill but I know better. Cassia's not shy when it comes to confiding in me and to her, Nigel, is a pleasant, temporary, distraction.

She's almost a full year younger than me, and at twenty, the last thing on her mind is a wedding. Unfortunately, it's the only thing on Nigel's mind which is why he's scheduled this discussion which I tried in vain to avoid by going for a run at the break of dawn.

"I couldn't sleep," he confesses as he takes a seat on the white sofa. "I've been too nervous."

I walk into the open kitchen. "I'm going to get a bottle of water. Do you want something?"

"I want you to go with me to pick out an engagement ring."

My hand stops in mid-air as I reach into the refrigerator. I suck a deep breath into my lungs. I don't want to be in the middle of this. I'd done that too many times in high school when Cassia couldn't find the nerve to break up with the guys she was seeing.

She'd call me crying, begging me to be the one to call her boyfriends to dump them.

I'd always refused, and each time instead of doing the decent thing, she'd fade slowly into the distance, ending things by ignoring the boys she once claimed to love.

A wedge was driven between us when I exploded one day, screaming at her for being heartless. We stopped talking for months after that, but then early one Tuesday morning when my life changed forever, she came over to my house and held me. She's still holding me in her own way and I'm still trying to guide her to consider the hearts of the men who fall in love with her too easily.

"You don't want to buy a ring right now," I finally say as I twist open the lid of the water bottle. "Why not wait until her birthday?"

"That's months from now," he points out. "I can't wait that long."

I take a large gulp of the water, holding it in my mouth before I swallow, hopeful that the silence in the room will be enough to send him back into the comfort of Cassia's bed. It doesn't work.

"I need you to help me with this, Isla." He cradles his forehead in his palms. "If I don't ask her and things change, I'll regret it forever."

There it is. Doubt. He senses it.

It's not surprising given the fact that Cassia hasn't been spending nearly the same amount of time with him now as she was six months ago, when they first started dating. Back then, she couldn't shut up about how perfect Nigel was. Now, most of the time, his name is only mentioned when she tells me she's unsure of what she really wants.

One day he's in the way. The next, when she doesn't hear from him for hours, she's texting him non-stop and I'm avoiding coming home for fear of hearing the two of them having sex in her room. She doesn't want him half of the time and she's all over him the other half. All I can do is keep enough distance from them both so I'm not dragged into the middle. I'm trying to do that now, but Nigel isn't making it easy.

"Will you go with me to look at rings? I've got time tomorrow."

"I'm busy tomorrow," I blurt back without considering my schedule. "Cassia's not big on surprises. Think about that before you do anything."

"Sure," he says sullenly. "I'll think about it."

I breathe a deep sigh of relief as I watch him stand up, walk down the hallway and disappear into the darkness of Cassia's room.

***

"What did you and Mr. Foster talk about after I left his office? It was about me, wasn't it?"

Yes, Cicely, of course it was. What else could the hottest man I've ever seen want to talk about other than you and your wardrobe which seems to take on a more unsightly tone by the day?

"The weather," I shoot back as I give her a once over. I had hoped that my eyes were playing sleepy tricks on me when I walked into the boutique twenty minutes ago but that is indeed a multicolored pantsuit paired with green ankle boots. She looks like a rainbow hit a tree full force.

I opted for a short, floral print dress and teal heels. I'm going to have to up my game if I want a customer's attention today. The three that have entered the boutique since I started my shift have all stopped to actually stare at Cicely.

"The weather?" she parrots back as she cocks both brows. "Mr. Foster doesn't strike me as the kind of man who talks about trivial things. Besides, why would I have to leave if you two were talking about that? I know it was about me."

Her ego train has obviously left the station and is barreling down the track at breakneck speed. I'm guessing the fuel behind that is the fact that Mr. Foster called ten minutes ago to tell her about a new promotion he wants to launch next month.

I'd overheard the conversation, or at least Cicely's side of it. Her voice had taken on a higher lilt. She'd listened intently and then had asked a series of short questions before thanking him for the call. The smile that lit up her face when she turned back towards me irked me in a way it shouldn't have.

Cicely is a Liore lifer. It's obvious that she plans on building her career here so I shouldn't fault her for doing her job well. I need to check my attitude if I'm going to chart a new course. I want this job for the foreseeable future so I need to do what's necessary and that includes obeying her rules. She is, after all, my boss.

"What are you doing the last Wednesday of the month?" Her words halt me just as I'm about to round the counter to walk towards a customer who is giving a display of silk panties a second glance.

"What? You mean on the 30th?" I turn back so I'm facing her.

She nods softly. "You're only scheduled until three that afternoon. I'm supposed to work until store closing but I need to switch."

I study her face, wondering if she's testing me. It doesn't matter if she is or not, I'm busy that night. "I'm sorry, Cicely. I can't. I have plans. "

I see something flash across her expression. I can't place it since it disappears too quickly. "I have plans too. Mine are with Mr. Foster."

If she's expecting any reaction out of me, I'm not going to give it to her. I stand stoic even though my mind is racing. Gabriel Foster is into Cicely? If I'd bet money on that, I would have lost. She doesn't strike me as his type, but what do I know?

"I'll ask someone else." She looks over my shoulder. "I don't want to disappoint Mr. Foster. He's looking forward to it."

I'm sure he is. I have no idea why he'd be looking forward to it, but to each his own, as they say.

"You should get out on the floor, Isla." Her fingers wave past my head. "There are customers waiting."

I glance in the direction of her hand towards a middle-aged man holding a bra at arm's length, his Rolex peeking out from under the arm of his suit jacket. I smile as I walk straight towards him knowing that by the time he leaves the store, I'll have made half my month's rent.

CHAPTER EIGHT

Gabriel

"Who are you screwing these days?"

I don't need to look up to know who is standing in the doorway of my office. It's the same question he's asked me since we were teenagers living in a cramped brownstone. He was as brash and unreserved then as he is now. The fact that he recently got married hasn't muted him at all. Caleb, my younger brother, will never change.

"Close the door." My eyes stay trained on my tablet.

"It's not that woman in accounting, is it?" he asks brusquely as he slams the doors behind him. "When I was down there last week I caught a glimpse of her computer and you, my dear brother, are her screen saver."

"I'm what?" I finally look up. "Who?"

"I don't know her name." He lowers himself into one of the chairs in front of my desk. "She's a redhead with squirrely eyes. She's in the cubicle near the elevator on the third floor."

"I'm not familiar," I say through a grin. "I'm her screensaver?"

He nods. "It's a picture of you dressed in a tux. She must have lifted it off the corporate website. You're looking good in it. I bet she trips the switch looking at that when everyone else in her department leaves for the day."

"Trips the switch?" I cock a brow.

"You know, she flicks the bean, double clicks the mouse. You're her man candy when she's …"

"Shut up." I literally shudder at the thought. I don't have a clue which employee he's referring to but I'm not oblivious to the glances that some of the women who work in the building throw me when I walk into the lobby every morning. Beyond that, it's not uncommon to have a woman press her body into mine during a crowded elevator ride.

I was witness to the same thing happening with Caleb. It still does, to a degree, but a lot has changed since he married Rowan Bell, my second-in-charge within the Liore division.

"How's Bell?" I ask, not only because she's been in Europe for almost a month, but the truth is I adore her. I view her as a younger sister. It makes sense given the fact that she lived next door to us when we were all children.

"Miserable without me." A broad smile takes over his mouth. "You need to tell her to get her ass back here, Gabriel. I miss her."

I miss her too. I can count my close friends on one hand and Bell is near the top of the list. I shield her from the things I don't want the world to know about me but beyond that I'm close to her. I was thrilled when she agreed to leave her last job to come work for me. She's as determined as I am to make Liore a success which is the main reason she's so skilled at handling the day-to-day operations.

"She'll be back at the end of the week. I assume she already told you that."

"She did." He leans back in the chair, crossing his legs. "You didn't answer my question."

"What question?"

"Who are you hooking up with lately?" He taps his fingers along the arm of the chair. "I heard you're bringing someone to the benefit at the end of the month."

"You heard wrong." I tip my chin in his direction. "I've invited a few employees from our stores. It's a good marketing move. It shows how much we care about the community."

"Is the cute blonde who was racing out of your office the other night one of those employees?" I lean back, crossing my arms over my chest. "She's not invited."

He looks past me towards the windows at the expansive view of Manhattan. "I was waiting for the elevator. She practically ran me over to get in it before me. What's her name?"

"Why?" I snap back, too quickly, too tersely.

"Woah." His hands shoot up in mock surrender. "I'm not chasing her. I'm married, remember?"

"How can I forget? You remind me at every chance that I'll never find a woman as perfect as the one you married."

"I've seen the blonde before." His mouth twists into a scowl. "I've tried to figure it out since then. I know her from somewhere."

"She works at the Liore boutique on Fifth Avenue."

"I've never set foot in there." He leans forward in the chair. "I must be mistaking her for someone else. There are a lot of cute blondes in New York."

I swipe my finger across the screen of my tablet, pulling up a series of images of ties from the men's upcoming spring line. He came here to talk business, not to discuss Isla Lane. She may be a beautiful blonde who I'm aching to fuck, but she's an employee. She's off-limits and though the challenge is tempting, the consequences aren't.

I'm going to find exactly what I want tonight.

For just a few hours I need a woman who is gorgeous, eager, and whose limits line up with mine.

***

"She's nothing like most of the girls who come here. She's different."

That's improbable.

It's also inconsequential.

I came to the club tonight for one purpose. If that purpose comes in the form of a woman that Sage thinks is one-of-a-kind, so be it. I'm not here to cast judgment. No one who sets foot in this club is. We're all here for the same reasons, to fuck or to be fucked, to control or to acquiesce.

The only difference between any of us is the thick, glass barrier that separates the seasoned club members from those who are curious. There's also the matter of the confidentiality agreement you sign when you're invited to cross the threshold into the private area of Club Skyn.

Discretion is paramount and, fortunately, legally required.

I rub elbows with many of New York City's elite here. Not one of them wants their predilections to follow them into the world outside these walls. I'm no different.

"You've barely touched your drink, Gabriel." Sage raises her near empty glass to toast. "Here's to you finally jumping back into the fray."

I nod slightly, my hand firmly clutching the glass of scotch I ordered shortly after I arrived. As soon as Caleb had left my office with instructions in hand for the tie collection, I'd hit the gym to spar with Landon Beckett, an old friend. I was restless and wanted to blow off the pent up energy before I showered.

Like Caleb, his life has settled into a pattern of predictability with a woman he's passionate about. I doubt he'd understand my need to be here. I doubt most people in my inner circle would.

I've never cared about that. I've never sought the approval of anyone when it comes to what I do after work, on my own hours. This is my life. These are my needs. This is what I thirst for and tonight I'm here to quench that.

"She's there." Sage's fingers paint an invisible trail along the glass.

I move closer, my eyes honing in on the crowded mass on the dance floor directly in front of us. Some of them know that there are others with a clear and uncensored view of what they're doing. Others, those who are new to Skyn, think that it's exactly as advertised, just another club on the Lower

East Side of the city. They're oblivious to the fact that the mirrored wall that runs the length of the dance floor becomes something more three nights a week.

It's on those nights that the large rooms behind the wall come to life with a fully stocked bar, music, and people who all want the same thing. From behind the one way glass we can assess, yearn for, and finally invite someone back to a place where consent is readily given and real names are rarely exchanged.

For those of us who understand the need for the private rooms equipped with all the tools of both pleasure and pain, we're here for one reason and one reason only.

"Where?" I lean closer to Sage hopeful that my voice will rise above the increasing volume of the rhythmic beat of the music that fills the entire club.

She taps her hand against the glass. "That's her. She's wearing a red dress. Her hair is long, it's brown. She's almost as tall as I am."

I scan the dance floor. I spot the woman Sage is pointing to almost immediately. Her dress, a scarlet red, hugs her frame. She's tall, lithe and has the body of a dancer. She's timid, her eyes darting from one side of the room to the other, all the while avoiding anyone.

"She's eager to meet you. I told her about you."

Those details would have been sparse at best. Sage, like anyone with an invitation to this area of the club, values her privacy. She's not going to willingly risk her reputation as the face of one of the country's most successful skin care lines.

Since the episode in my office years ago, she's been discreet. I don't trust her fully. I never will but I recognize her need to be in the public eye. Her brand is what motivates her to keep her own secrets, as well as mine, hidden.

"What's her name?" I ask, as I turn back to look at the brunette. I don't expect an answer grounded in truth. I don't care what her real name is. I'll call her whatever she wants me to tonight because when I walk out of this club, I know that the driving need I feel right now will be quieted. I also know that by the time I feel the urge again, I'll be in Italy on business, or Germany, or somewhere, anywhere, far away from here.

"It's…"

Sage's voice is drowned out. It's not the music, or the boisterous sound of the voices next to us that overtakes me. It's my breathing. It's my own labored breathing.

I still as my eyes wander from the woman Sage pointed out to another, across the floor from her. Although her back is turned to me, the attraction is instant and intense.

I spot her legs first. They're not long, but they're toned. They disappear beneath a thin piece of black silk which only serves to cover the curves of a flawlessly shaped ass. The back of the halter dress she's wearing is non-existent revealing a smooth, delicately angled back.

As she turns slightly, the ponytail her hair is pulled into sways with the movement and the silver hoop earring in her left ear bounces against her neck. Even beneath the muted lighting above the dance floor there's no mistaking the outline of her full breasts beneath the fabric of the dress. She's supple, sensual and even though I've yet to see her face, she's undeniably, the most beautiful woman in the room.

"Gabriel." I feel Sage's hand on my shoulder. "Did you hear me? I said her name is Jovie."

"Not her." I stare at the woman in the short black dress. "I don't want Jovie. She's not the one."

"She is the one." Her voice is insistent. "I've spoken to her. We had a drink the other night. She's perfect."

"No. I found the one I want."

"Who?" Her tone is clipped and severe.

I feel my cock harden as the woman I can't take my eyes off of starts to move to the music. The fabric of her dress brushes against her ass tempting anyone within view. I see the blatant hungry glances of the men around her. I watch as they move closer, circling her like the untamed animals they are.

Not one of them is going to touch that body, taste it, or satisfy it the way I will.

I motion towards one of the club managers who are here to facilitate the needs of the people in this room. Their job is to go out and test the waters. They speak to the club patrons who have caught the eye of a private member. If the interest is mutual, they take them to a lounge, instruct them on protocol and handle all the necessary paperwork that ensures what happens here, stays here.

I adjust the buckle of my belt before my hand lightly grazes over the front of my pants. I'm so hard that there's a bite of pain. This is exactly what I need. She's what I need.

"Is there someone you'd like to meet?"

The older man who approaches me doesn't use my name even though we've lunched together within the realm of my business. "The one in the short black dress, silver heels, hoop earrings."

He glances past me towards the wall of glass, his hand rising in the air. "That one, sir?"

I turn back towards the dance floor and as my eyes hone in on her again, my hand fists. She's facing me directly now, her neck tilted slightly to the left as she talks to a blonde haired man I've seen back here, behind the shroud of glass. He's a regular and as she looks up into his eyes, my stomach recoils.

It's then that I see her stumble against him and as she glances towards where I'm standing, hidden behind the glass wall, there's no mistaking the glossy look in her blue eyes.

"Is that the one, sir? It's the blonde?"

"Get yourself another drink." I turn towards Sage. "I need a moment."

She nods absentmindedly as she walks off in the direction of the bar.

I level my eyes on the manager. "You have a problem."

He chuckles nervously. "I have a problem?"

"That woman is underage."

"That's impossible." He moves closer to the glass until his nose is hovering next to it. "We have a stringent policy regarding proper identification. It would have been checked at the door."

"It's possible," I hiss. "In fact, it's reality. That woman is twenty-years-old. She's also clearly intoxicated."

"I'm not sure how this happened." He pulls a smartphone from his pocket. "I'll have security remove her."

"You'll have a female manager quietly lead her out before she escorts her home."

"We don't have enough staff…"

"It's not a request." I glance back to where Isla is standing, her arms now around the neck of the man she's talking to. "Take care of it now or I'll call Julian to handle it."

The mention of the club's owner is enough to light a fire under the manager. As he walks away I turn back towards the dance floor. I bring the glass in my hand to my lips, take a heavy drink and curse under my breath as I wonder what the fuck Isla Lane is doing in this club.

CHAPTER NINE

Isla

"You'll need to come with me."

I ignore her at first, not because I'm rude. At least, I try not to be rude. I don't pay any attention to her because I'm sure she's talking to the woman next to me who has been flashing her tits at some guy parked on a bar stool.

I see a lot of breasts in my line of work. On any given day I'd venture to guess that I see at least four or five pairs when I'm helping customers try on bras.

I don't compare them to mine because I know mine are spectacular. I'm not conceited. It's just that every guy I've ever fucked has said the same thing.

Well, I mean they've said other things, like I'm good at oral or I'm too loud when I come but for the most part, they've liked my breasts. I like them too.

"Excuse me." I feel a light tap on my shoulder with the words.

The tone is too high to be Barry's. Besides he's staring at me and he hasn't said anything for at least two minutes. I think he asked me something. Did he ask me something?

I feel sick. Like so sick right now.

"I'd like you to come with me." I hear the voice again. It's definitely a woman.

I look to my left and I see her there. She's dressed all in black. Even her dark hair is pulled back into a bun. She's the exact opposite of fun. She's no fun. I wonder if she's related to Cicely.

I think I might vomit.

"She's not going anywhere with you. I'm taking this one to the back with me," Barry, the blonde haired dentist I met earlier, says really loudly. He says it so loudly that my head hurts.

"There's a problem, sir." The grumpy lady is pulling on my arm. "I'm going to have to escort her from the club."

"That's not happening." Barry grabs hold of my waist. "We are going to the back. I've invited her and she accepted."

Technically I haven't exactly RSVP'd yet. He did invite me when he was kissing my neck and drooling in my ear. I was leaning more towards not going. He's not my type and I haven't flossed today so we're not a good match. I know how much dentists hate it when you don't floss. My grandmother always said that if you can't say something nice, try and say something nice…no wait, if you can't say something nice, say something not nice? No…it was…

"You're a good dancer." I tap my hand on his chest. "I like dancing with you."

"What's the problem?" Barry ignores my compliment. "I don't understand what the problem is." "There's an issue with her identification." The woman gestures towards my clutch purse.

"What issue?" Barry's voice is even louder now. I definitely have a headache.

"Shh." I bring my finger to my lips. "You're so loud."

The woman in the dark clothes leans close to us both. "We have reason to believe she used fake identification to get into the club."

Well, shit. I am so fucking busted right now.

I pull my clutch closer. That fake ID cost me a lot and I need it at least for the next ten days until I'm actually twenty-one. I don't want this woman to take it away from me. What if I decide I need a drink after work one day?

Who am I kidding? After tonight, I'm never drinking again.

"Her ID is legit," Barry says.

"Don't say legit." I grimace as I look up into his face and shake my head from side-to-side. "It's not cool, Barry. You're like over that hill, you know what I mean?"

The woman talking to us stifles a laugh.

"Give me that ID." Barry grabs hold of my clutch so quickly that I don't have time to react. A lot of that has to do with the two, wait, it was three vodkas and sodas I've had since I got here.

"I want it back." I try to yank the bag back into my hands. "That's mine."

"Sir, you need to step back." A man dressed in a dark suit is standing next to us now. I recognize his bald head. I saw it when I first came into the club. He was greeting some people at the door.

"He took my bag," I whine. "Tell him to give it back."

I pull harder on the clutch but Barry's got it in a death grip. He's shaking his head and gritting his teeth. "I'll show you that her ID is real. She's at least twenty-five. Look at her."

61

I pull harder. "You think I'm twenty-five? Really? I look twenty-five to you?"

"At least." Barry pushes the bald headed man aside as he tugs on my clutch. "Just tell them the ID is real so we can go to the back."

"No." I shake my head as I let the clutch go. "It's not real. I'm only twenty. I won't be twenty-one for another ten days."

I don't see Barry's expression as he falls on his ass. My eyes are glued to my clutch and as it flies out of his grasp and through the air, I say a silent prayer that the broken clasp will hold tight.

It doesn't.

All I can do is cover my eyes as the contents of my clutch spill out and into the view of virtually everyone in the room who has stopped to stare at the commotion we caused. I hear the faints gasps and giggles as my phone, the six condoms, two ten dollar bills and the fake ID tumble to the floor right next to the brand new shiny handcuffs I brought with me.

***

"You look like shit, Isla."

If I'd bothered to look in a mirror today, I'd probably see it for myself. I've avoided it on purpose. In fact, this is the first time I've been up all day and I only got as far as the sofa.

I'd fallen into my bed right after I was dropped off. The woman from the club had not only walked me to the curb, she'd climbed into the front seat of a dark sedan that stopped on the street after she'd ushered me into the back.

I had given my address when asked, never questioning why I wasn't tossed from the club to fend for myself. It wasn't until I woke this morning that I realized that she had also helped me into the building and stayed with me until I closed my apartment door after thanking her for everything.

"I had too much to drink last night." I take a sip from the water bottle I've been holding in my hand for the past thirty minutes. "Do you have any aspirin?"

"I have something that will help." Cassia marches across the living room towards where she dropped her purse when she got home five minutes ago. "Did you have a date? Where did you go that you got so loaded?"

I went to a kinky club because I like to be handcuffed and spanked until my ass is on fire, Cass. What did you do last night?

"No date," I confess. "I haven't met anyone since I've been in New York."

Her brows perk up as she fishes a bottle of ibuprofen from out of her purse. "You haven't met anyone? I guess that makes sense. You work in a lingerie store. It must be all women, all the time."

It's not. At least half the customers are men either looking for something for their woman or men looking for someone to give them a free fashion show. "You wouldn't believe how many men come into Liore wanting to get off in the change rooms."

"You're kidding." Her voice explodes into the space, reverberating through my still sore brain. I swear even my eyelashes hurt today. I open the bottle and pop two pills into my mouth, using the last of the water to wash them down.

"I'm serious," I say quietly, hoping she'll take the hint and temper her tone. "It's happened to me a few times."

"You don't ever actually do it, do you? Tell me you don't."

I should be offended by the question but I can't be. Cassia knows me better than anyone. She was the one who laughed alongside me when I got caught in the art supply closet in high school with the captain of the debate team. We were only kissing but it was enough for yet another warning in my file.

"I don't," I say honestly. "It's against company policy. I wouldn't risk it."

"I'm surprised by how much you like this job." She walks into the kitchen. "I know it's just temporary but you're killing it there."

I am killing it. I got paid yesterday and with all the commissions I've earned, my check was the biggest it's ever been. If I didn't have any other direction for my life, I might stay at Liore for a year or two.

I can't let that happen though. I made a promise to myself and selling lingerie for the next three, or four, or more years of my life isn't part of that.

"Have you decided whether you're going to audition yet?" She walks back into the room carrying a glass of orange juice. "Here, drink this."

I tentatively take the glass from her hands as I look up at her face. Her olive skin is glowing. Her hazel eyes surrounded by long, beautiful lashes. She

rarely wears any make-up. She's never had to. Her
natural beauty rivals any woman I've ever met.

"No, not yet. I need more time to think about
it."

"There's a woman I work with at Hughes
Enterprises. I was telling her about you and…"

"You told her about me?" I interrupt. "What
did you tell her?"

"The regular stuff anyone would tell another
person about their best friend." She nervously shifts
from one foot to the other. "You have a lot in
common."

An involuntary smile pulls at the corners of
my mouth. "Does she play the violin too, like me?"

"No one plays the violin like you, Isla." She
rubs her hand across my forehead sweeping my hair
to the side. "If you audition for that opening with the
String Orchestra, you'll get that spot. Hell, if you tell
them who you are, they'll give you the spot without
you having to play a note."

I swallow hard. I know that she's trying to
help but she's not. It's in Switzerland. That's an entire
world away from my life here. "I'm not ready for that
yet. I need more time."

The sigh that escapes her is noticeable in the
stillness of the room. "I know. I just don't want you to
waste your talent. It's a gift, Isla. I know you can't see
it but it's true."

I do see it. That's because I spent the first
thirteen years of my life being paraded around the
globe like a show pony with a violin in hand. I was
my mother's meal ticket and she made it clear, in no

uncertain terms, that my talent was what was keeping our household afloat.

She resented the fact that when she was a child my grandmother, Ella Amherst, was focused on her career as the principal violinist with the London Philharmonic. My mother took it upon herself to rebel in every way possible, including getting pregnant with me, when she was still a teenager.

When the two of them finally settled in Chicago shortly after I was born, my grandmother took on a position with the Orchestra there. My mother took up with one man, and then another, and eventually I ended up with two younger half-sisters, and a handful of stepfathers.

My only solace through all the upheaval was the violin my grandmother had given me. She taught me how to play and with each invitation I received to appear on local television programs or radio stations, my mother's greed grew. Eventually, she was booking me to play at weddings, birthdays and even funerals.

I was the adorable blond haired girl with the big blue eyes and the talent of her grandmother. Nothing more than a novelty, drawing the attention of celebrities and royalty who thought it cute to throw the spotlight on a small child who could play classical music alongside many of the best musicians in the world.

As my bank account ballooned, my school work suffered and when I had to repeat seventh grade because the tutor my mother hired only existed on paper as a tax write-off, my grandmother stepped in.

She retired early, hired attorneys and accountants and when the dust settled and my trust accounts were searched, it was obvious to everyone that my mother's large house and her expensive car weren't paid for from her manager's salary. She'd stolen from me; money, time, my childhood.

I moved in with my grandmother then and after school each day, she'd insist I'd finish my homework first and then we'd play our violins, side-by-side, her helping me perfect my techniques. Those are the moments I'll treasure forever.

"You'll think about auditioning, Isla. Promise me you will." Cassia's hands rest on my shoulders.

"I'll think about it. I promise."

CHAPTER TEN

Gabriel

"If I need to get my attorney involved in this, I will."

It's meant to sound as threatening as it does. It's also proven to be an effective way to deal with the hordes of individuals who believe they can produce imitation, substandard products, and sell them with fake Arilia or Berdine labels attached to them.

"No, please, no sir." The small, seemingly meek looking, man stares up at me. "I didn't know. I'll give them all to you. You can take them now."

That would solve all of his problems. Unfortunately, it would only prolong the inevitable. If I gather up the dozens of men's dress shirts and the handful of women's blouses he has on display, it will only put a dent in his business for at most a day, or two.

These portable carts, hawking imitation merchandise, are as much a part of the landscape of the streets of Manhattan as those selling hotdogs and pretzels. The only difference is that the food vendors are earning an honest living.

He can play coy all he wants but I've seen this happen time and time again.

"I'll send someone down to deal with this within the hour." I turn on my heel ignoring his pleading offerings to keep the police out of it.

I will.

All I need is the threat of a lawsuit delivered in the form of one of the company's staff of attorneys to ensure that nothing bearing any of the Foster fashion brands lands on this cart again.

I make a quick call to the head of the legal department of Foster Enterprises, apprising her of the situation, including the location of the cart which ironically is set up less than a block from my office.

As I end the call, I hear the unmistakable chime of a bell signaling a new test message.

I look down at the screen of my phone, read the message and curse under my breath.

What the fuck is this?

I walked to a local bodega to get a cup of coffee to clear my head. I needed fresh air and a break from a day that has been filled with nothing but mundane problems that feel like a waste of my time.

Now, another issue is pressing and since my driver is at least fifteen minutes away, I do the only thing I can think of. I toss the paper cup in the trash, wave my hand in the air and flag down the first passing taxi to take me to the Liore boutique.

***

It's the most erotic instance of déjà vu I've ever experienced.

As I walk through the door of the boutique my eyes instantly gravitate toward Isla. She's near the back of the space with a female customer.

Her hair is different today. It's wavy, as if she let it dry on its own before she ran her fingers through the golden locks. Her dress is pale blue, fitted and framed in lace. She looks innocent and angelic. She looks nothing like she did three nights ago at Skyn when she was escorted from the club.

I'd left the private room and had stood in the shadows listening to her speak with the female manager who had been sent to accompany her home. She was sweet, sexy, and irresistible as she tried to wrestle her clutch purse away from an asshole that had no right to be near her.

I'd watched in both horror and fascination as her clutch opened revealing everything she'd tucked inside it before she'd arrived at the club.

The condoms and money were expected. The handcuffs caught me off guard.

I haven't touched a pair since college when I'd used them on a woman I met at a club similar to Skyn. She was sure it was what she wanted but when she'd heard the click of the metal closing around her wrists and I parted her legs to fuck her, she'd panicked.

I fumbled with the key as I unlocked her, trying to comfort her but the slap across my face had stilled everything.

She'd left my dorm room in a huff with the handcuffs still attached to one of the posts of my bed frame. I'd tossed them in the trash along with her number.

I prefer softer restraints. Fabrics that have enough give to allow a woman to feel comfortable, yet enough strength to hold her exactly where I want her to be.

Isla's preference is metal. Although judging by the condition of her handcuffs as they hit the floor a few feet from where I was standing, they've rarely been used, if at all.

That might speak to her experience or lack thereof. Either way, it's becoming harder to ignore her.

"Mr. Foster, you're finally here."

I look to my right to where Cicely is standing, her voice conveying the same panic that her text message had.

"Cicely, the building isn't on fire. I don't see anyone with a weapon demanding money." I gesture towards the crowded sales floor. "If there's an emergency here, I'm not seeing it."

"I didn't mean it was that kind of emergency, sir." She's wringing the pair of lace panties within her knotted fists so tightly that I wouldn't be surprised if they ripped in two.

"Don't manhandle the merchandise."

"I tried calling Wallis but it goes straight to voicemail." She sighs heavily as her eyes survey the boutique. "I found something in one of the change rooms. I don't know what to do with it."

I have no idea why I didn't call her before I raced to the boutique. Actually, that's a lie. I know why. The reason is blonde, effortlessly beautiful and now bent over to retrieve a bra that the customer she's helping has dropped. I wanted to see Isla.

"Will you look at it?"

"Look at what?" I can't pull my gaze from Isla. She's laughing. Her eyes dancing over the face of the woman she's helping. It's obvious why she sells more product than any other sales associate in this store. She's captivating. Who in their right mind could walk away from her?

"It's in the back office, sir." Cicely's hand rests on my forearm. "I'll show it to you now."

I turn my head to look at her hand. "I don't have time for this. You're the manager. Your job is to handle anything and everything that involves this store."

"I know. I do. I just don't know how to deal with this."

"Are you like this with Rowan?" I ask out of sheer frustration.

Foster Enterprises employs thousands worldwide. Each of those people has to report to someone above them within the company's hierarchy. For Cicely, that's Rowan Bell and right now, I'm cursing the fact that I sent her to Europe at all. She should be back here, holding Cicely's hand to get her through this latest non-crisis.

"Like what?"

"Exactly what am I doing here?" I pull my arm free so I can turn to face her directly. "I can't imagine what you found that warrants me dropping everything to come down here."

"I can't say it, sir." She blushes as she looks up at me. "Can you please just come with me so I can show you?"

"Fine," I snap. Unless I give this woman what she wants, which amounts to even more of my time, she's not going to leave this be.

I follow her through the store, my eyes locking briefly with Isla's as I offer a simple greeting to the customer she's helping. Although I want nothing more than to stop to speak with Isla, I don't. I need to see what has Cicely in knots so I can get to the first of several meetings I have scheduled this afternoon.

"It's right over here, sir." Cicely marches across the tiled floor of the cramped office to a wastebasket sitting next to a plain metal desk covered in invoices, order forms and schedules.

"What is over here?" I stop to glance down at my smartphone in my palm.

"That." Her hand darts into the air towards the wastebasket. "I found that on the floor in one of the change rooms an hour ago."

I shake my head as I move towards her, my eyes glued to her face. "We hired you for this position because of your background in retail, Cicely. Unless you can show more leadership and take more control over this store, I'm going to discuss an alternative arrangement with Rowan."

The expression on her face doesn't shift at all and I realize she likely didn't hear anything I just said. Her hand is bobbing in the air right above the wastebasket.

I drop my gaze, lean forward and look in.
"You found that in a change room?"
She nods briskly. "I found it an hour ago, sir."
"Who was working then? Who was here?"

Her bottom lip quivers slightly. "It was just me and Isla. We were the only two here."

I stare at the used condom and the empty foil packet. It's the same brand that fell from Isla's clutch and littered the floor of the club.

CHAPTER ELEVEN

Isla

I saw Mr. Foster checking me out when he walked into the boutique twenty minutes ago.

Checking me out may be too strong of words, or more likely, wishful thinking.

I did notice him staring in my direction. It may have had everything to do with the fact that I didn't have enough time to straighten my hair after my shower. I'm a mess. I overslept this morning and being late isn't something I can afford to do right now.

I can't screw up again. Mr. Foster made that very clear.

"Isla, I need a word."

My head pops up at the harsh clipped sound of Mr. Foster's voice. He's standing in front of the counter, not more than two feet away from where I am. Cicely is next to him, her arms folded across her chest.

I'm in shit. Real shit this time.

"Of course, sir," I say in the most sincere tone I can muster. "Can someone take over for me?"

Cicely looks around the store. "Steph started ten minutes ago. I'll get her to watch the register."

I nod as I stand in place, my eyes focused completely on Mr. Foster. He's wearing a black shirt and suit today. The only contrast is the silver tie around his neck. He's polished, calm and judging by the way he's looking at me, he's not going to be as understanding as he was last time.

Lucky for me, I haven't broken any rules since then; at least, none that I know of.

"We'll do this in the office." He steps away from the counter just as Steph, another sales associate, comes into view. "Follow me."

I do as I'm told. My heels drumming a fast beat against the tiled floor as I fall in step behind him. I don't turn to look but I know instinctively that Cicely is pulling up the rear of this train of doom.

She'd looked panicked when she went to retrieve garments from the fitting rooms earlier. I'd stopped her to ask a question but she'd brushed me off with a shake of her head and a hand in the air to silence me.

I hadn't pushed. I've been working for her long enough to know that when she's on a mission, it's best to get the hell out of her way. I did that by focusing on customers and doing what I was hired to do.

"Close the door, Cicely."

My stomach knots instantly when I hear the brash tone of his voice. Something is definitely wrong. This job is becoming way more trouble than it's worth.

I hear the latch of the door as it's closed. I stand quiet, waiting for him to speak.

"You had intercourse in one of the change rooms this morning." Cicely's anxious voice breaks the silence. "I know it was you."

Mr. Foster cocks a dark brow as his eyes jump to my face. I can't tell what his reaction is. He's silent save for the faint tapping of his shoe against the floor.

"What?" I shake my head from side-to-side as Cicely moves into view. "I didn't. I wouldn't."

"You did." She reaches towards a wastebasket. "I found a used… there was a used thing in there. I found the package too."

"A used thing? A condom?" I search her face trying to find something there that resembles even a shred of sanity. I've been well within her view all morning. I've been on the sales floor, helping one customer and then another. "I haven't been in the change rooms. It wasn't me. It was someone else."

"Well it wasn't me," she spits the words out. "I checked the rooms before I opened the store the same way I do every morning and there was nothing there. There were no garments leftover from when customers tried things on yesterday and there were no... nothing else was in that room. That means that you took a man in there so you could do stuff with him."

Stuff? Grow the fuck up, Cicely and just spit it out. You think I fucked some random in the change room.

"Mr. Foster," I say his name quietly realizing that I need to appeal directly to him. Cicely has already convicted me of being a shameless slut. "I didn't do this. I know the rules."

His full lips part slightly before he runs the tip of his index finger over his eyebrow. "We've already had this discussion, Isla. You don't always follow all the rules."

I suck in a slow, deep breath as his eyes fall from my face to the top of my dress. "I didn't break that rule. I wouldn't take a man into a change room with me."

"Do you have any idea who would?" he rasps. "If it wasn't Cicely or you, explain to me who had that access."

I can't. The doors are locked until an employee unlocks them. It's a measure that's in place to deter theft. We know exactly what items go into each room and we have to account for what comes out. We're also not allowed to let men go back there to see their wives or girlfriends trying on the merchandise.

"I don't know. All I know is it wasn't me."

"Are you saying it was me?" Cicely's hands jump to the waist of her purple dress. "Do you think it was me, Isla?"

I look her over from head to toe. "Of course not. No one would think it was you."

Her eyes squint. "What does that mean?"

I don't have to explain it. I can't explain it. It hasn't slipped my mind that Cicely and Mr. Foster have a date next Friday night. I'm not about to insult her with him standing less than a foot away from me.

"I've been on the sales floor since I got here." I look down at my hands, twisting them together in frustration. "I wasn't near the change rooms at all today."

"You didn't let any of the customers in the rooms?" Cicely says in a tone that is way too judgmental. "You're telling me that not one of your customers wanted to try anything on?"

I turn towards her, my patience wearing thin. "I spent time with two customers this morning." I dart two fingers in the air. "One was a woman who wanted to buy new bras for her mother who just had a double mastectomy and reconstructive surgery. She knew the size. It's a perfect 34C. My other customer was in here last week. Her husband loved the things she bought so much that she came back for more so she could surprise him on their anniversary. Neither of them needed to go to the rooms."

Cicely's eyes move from my face to Mr. Foster's.

"There are security cameras," I think aloud. "I've seen Wallis watching the footage when she caught a shoplifter. There aren't any in the rooms but they do give a view of who goes in and out of them."

"I was just about to suggest that." Cicely turns towards the door. "I remember Wallis mentioning those. We can review them right now to prove what really happened."

"I need to go." I don't make eye contact with either of them. "I have customers waiting for me."

I brush past Cicely, twist the doorknob in my hand, and walk back to the front of the boutique knowing that as soon as I can, I'm leaving this fucked up circus behind me for good.

CHAPTER TWELVE

Gabriel

The water pounds down on me. The heated spray beating a path along my back. My eyes are closed. My mind is too awake. It's near three in the morning and I haven't slept. I can't quiet my thoughts.

The full day of work I had planned ended abruptly as I watched the security tapes in the Liore boutique. I'd called Wallis to the store from the corporate offices to assist me. She'd been in a meeting, an important meeting, regarding the men's line.

My better judgement was swept aside by my insatiable, unexplainable need, to see who had fucked who in that change room.

When Cicely had showed me that condom package and the refuse of what had transpired in the cramped space, I'd been hit with images of Isla bent over the bench, her dress hiked to her waist, her panties pushed aside as a customer pounded his dick into her from behind.

I'd imagined his hand bunched in her hair, pulling her neck back as he rode her fast and hard. The sense of rage I felt with those thoughts invading my mind was palpable. It wasn't rational but it was real and stifling.

She'd looked different when her eyes met mine in the boutique. I saw a need and a desire there that I hadn't before. It may have been nothing more than my remembrances of how she looked in the club. She was so ripe, willing, and waiting to be taken.

My intention when she followed me into the office was clear. I wanted a simple explanation. I wanted her assurance that she wasn't the one who had taken a man into that space. I needed to know that. It had nothing to do with her job. It had everything to do with my selfish need to slide my cock inside of her.

I felt relief wash over me when Wallis spotted the culprits on the footage. The cleaning crew had granted themselves carte blanche in the boutique hours before the store opened. The man and his female counterpart, hired to clean the store, had instead fucked like rabbits in the corridor leading to the change room before they fell out of view and into the room.

Cicely's explanation for not finding the evidence of their misdeeds when she did her required check of the rooms before the store's opening was far reaching. She'd been interrupted mid-check she claimed at first by a customer knocking on the door, wanting early access to the sales items.

As Wallis ran through the security footage one final time, Cicely's story lost all merit. It was clear that she'd strolled through the corridor before the store opened, unlocking each of the change room doors before pushing them open with a brush of her foot as her eyes were cast down at her smartphone. She was blissfully unaware that cameras were even in place.

When I finally walked through the boutique on my way out two hours later, Isla's back was turned to me. I'd stopped to thank her for being so cooperative but the only response was a faint nod of her head before she walked to the left to adjust a row of stockings that had been knocked astray by the greedy hands of bargain hunters.

She's pissed. I don't blame her. Cicely fucked up and I was pulled into that.

That's not who I am.

It's not who I want to be.

I don't care if a woman I'm interested in fucks someone else. I'll find another.

I don't care if a woman I want tells me to go to hell.

I move on. I find someone else. I fuck her until I forget everyone else and then I walk away.

That's who I am.

It's who I want to be.

The only difference now is that I know Isla Lane exists and I can't get her out of my mind.

***

"You can't possibly be mad at either of them, Gabriel." My mother hugs me gently taking care not to allow her face to touch mine. From the looks of it, she's spent hours in someone's make up chair. "Caleb and Rowan were waiting for me. I wanted to look my best."

She looks stunning.

I'm not surprised. Whenever there's a spotlight to be had, or a red carpet to stand on, my mother will be front and center. Tonight she's wearing a striking royal blue dress from one of our boutiques. It's cut just low enough to show off a stunning diamond necklace. I'm not about to ask where it came from. We'll have that discussion when her credit card bill crosses my desk in a few weeks.

"I'm not angry," I say quietly hoping to diffuse her. If the cameras aren't pointed at her, she'll do whatever is necessary to draw them towards her. Once, three or four years ago, she burst out in song during a press event for the Berdine line. It took months of negotiating, manipulating and subtle coercion to get the gossip rags to finally move on to another story.

At the time, my mother viewed their ongoing attention as flattery. I knew better. They would follow her in hopes of catching her in another moment of desperation. Things have calmed now, but I work hard to keep her in the background, out of the way of any stray microphones or cameras.

Tonight, I'm grateful that they've focused all of their attention on Libby Duncan, the Broadway actress, who is thankfully wearing a red, strapless dress from the Arilia collection. Her picture will be splashed across countless papers and websites tomorrow morning and that dress will be sold out within hours. That's the type of publicity that is priceless.

"I had hoped that Caleb would be here to present the check." I glance over to where my brother and his wife are standing, engaged in a lively conversation with the orchestra's conductor. "I took care of it. I'm just glad you're here in time for the performance."

"I've never been to the symphony, Mr. Foster."

I turn toward the female voice. It's Cicely, in a bright yellow dress. I make a mental note to talk to Caleb about offering our employees a stipend that includes free merchandise from each of our boutiques. A visit to Arilia would benefit Cicely and it wouldn't hurt our bottom line if she wore our designs to Liore each day. Cross promoting our own brands is a smart move.

Socializing with employees isn't something I'd normally do but this event is a benefit for an organization that promotes the arts for children. The chair is a close personal friend of my mother's and also the head partner at one of the most prestigious law firms in New York.

From its beginnings, he's been a robust supporter of the Foster Foundation, an organization founded by two of my cousins that provides medical care to individuals who have fallen on difficult times. Attending tonight, with a large check in hand, is a benefit for everyone.

"It's nice to see you, Cicely," I offer as I watch my mother walk towards Caleb.

She grabs hold of my hand, pulling it close to her. "I've never been at an event like this. I'm so honored that you asked me to join you."

My gaze follows the movement of my hand in hers. I jerk it away just as she's about to clasp it to her chest. "It's an important cause. It's vital that Foster Enterprises shows support. I'm glad that you, and the other employees, could make it."

She glances up at me, a wave of disappointment washing over her eyes. "I'm always happy to help the company in any way I can, sir."

I had asked her to attend this benefit, and the charity concert that immediately follows, on the phone, during an afternoon of similar calls to over a dozen employees.

I hadn't considered my choice of words at the time because I assumed that she'd understand that the invitation was offered in relation to her position at Liore. Not once did it cross my mind that she believed that the two of us would be attending this cocktail party before the symphony's performance as anything other than representatives of Foster Enterprises.

"Things are going well at the boutique," she blurts out, I assume, to change the subject. "You haven't come in since that day. I mean that day I found that trash."

It's been almost two weeks since I reviewed that security footage. It had taken all the restraint I possessed not to go back to the boutique after that day. I felt the pull on an almost hourly basis to walk in, under the guise of a short meeting with Cicely, just so I could see Isla.

It was type of temptation that is pure torture. The desire overwhelming, the need undefinable and the drive to listen to her voice, inhale her sweet scent and touch her is potent.

Once Rowan returned I'd delegated everything back to her, reminding her that she, and she alone, is responsible for the day-to-day operations of the Liore division.

She'd fallen back into step, speaking to Cicely about her management skills and spending time at the boutique to streamline their systems. Everything had calmed, even my unexplainable need to see Isla.

I had almost exploded at the boutique that day. My heart had pounded as I watched that footage, holding my breath with the hope that Isla wasn't fucking someone else. It made no sense. I have no claim to her.

I can't pull her into my world. I won't walk out of it the same. I can't risk that, not even for a woman like Isla.

"The performance is going to start soon, Gabriel." My mother taps my shoulder. "I want to freshen up before we take our seats. I'll find you in the concert hall."

No, she won't. She'll find a cocktail, and then another, and most likely someone more than willing to listen to her retell the story of what she deems her tortured youth back in Belgium. She'll never understand that having to fetch herself a glass of milk occasionally, when the private chef my grandparents employed was busy, is not the same as not having enough food to eat.

"I'll show you the way." I motion towards the doors that lead out of the reception hall and into the lobby of the venue. "I wouldn't want you to get misdirected. No good would come of that."

CHAPTER THIRTEEN

Isla

"Are you nervous?" I reach up to straighten the lapel of the tuxedo he's wearing. It's the second time I've seen him in it. He looks dashing. I'd told him that the first time and he'd laughed the way he does when he's embarrassed. "You look really nervous, Davis."

"A little," he confesses as he scoops my hand into his. "I wanted Derek to come with me tonight, but he had to work."

I sensed the disappointment in his eyes the moment I spotted him across the room. His partner, Derek, is the fountain of strength that he thinks he needs. He's wrong. I've known Davis Benoit for most of my life and I admire him more than anyone else.

Much of that has to do with his raw natural talent but there's also the fact that he's the most humble person I've ever met. I've watched him accept numerous awards and each time he is honored, he tells me that he's certain they've made a mistake. There's no mistake. Davis is brilliant and I'm very lucky that he's one of my closest friends.

"What time is it now?"

I glance down at my hands, realizing that I left my clutch with my phone inside back in the room I was directed to when I first arrived.

"Don't you have your phone?" I tap on his arm, before I point at the jacket he's wearing.

"I forgot mine at home. I was in a rush. Do you think I have time to use the washroom?"

I sigh heavily. I know that he needs to know the time not only so he can steal a few minutes away but so he can mentally prepare himself. We follow the same routine each and every time. The only difference is that usually Derek is nearby and he wears a watch.

I scan the area near us looking for a server. They always know the time and they're less likely to look down their noses at me when I ask. I don't see one so I take a few steps to the side, hoping one of them will pop into view.

I throw Davis a half-shrug before I start towards a couple standing a few feet away from us. They can't be much older than I am and when I first arrived, the woman had smiled at me. It was nothing more than a common act of decency but it felt generous to me.

I try to walk towards her but I'm quickly swallowed up the crowds. I look back but Davis has disappeared behind a wall of people I've never met.

"Isla Lane?"

The sound of a man's voice, combined with a light tap on my shoulder, stops me in my tracks. I search my mind, trying to place a face to the voice. It's deep, gruff and completely unfamiliar.

I turn on my heel and look up, my eyes quickly clouding with tears.

"Mr. Benoit," I say his name as he pulls me into his chest. "You came. I didn't think you'd make it."

"I can't resist an invitation from you. You asked and I delivered."

"Davis is going to be so excited." I playfully tap his shoulder as I look up at his kind face, now covered with a graying beard. "He has no idea you flew here from Chicago, does he?"

"I haven't said a word." His eyes leave mine to survey the people around us. "Where is he? Do I have time to talk to him now?"

I grab hold of his wrist and glance at the antique gold watch he's wearing. "You have time. He's near the box office. That's where I left him."

"You'll show me?" He extends his hand in front of him. "I want him to know it was your idea that I come tonight."

"I really need to use the ladies' room," I lie. "I'll catch up with you two in a few."

He nods as he walks away, gently pushing his way through the crowd. I stand in place wanting to give them at least a few moments together before I reappear. They need a chance to just be a dad and his son. I need the time to search out a glass of water to quench my thirst.

I look to the left for a server and just as I spot one, a man steps into my view. I stare at the meticulously crafted tuxedo he's wearing before my eyes travel up to his face and the beginnings of a beard covering his chin. The moment my gaze reaches his lips, my pulse quickens. It's him. Gabriel Foster, dressed to kill, is staring right at me.

***

"Perhaps you'd like something stronger to drink?"

I lick the water from my lips and hand the now empty glass back to him. "I'm fine now. Thank you."

He nods to the server as he places the glass tumbler back on her tray. I'd stopped her when she walked past me just after I spotted him across the lobby. I'd downed the water so quickly that a few drops had scattered onto the front of my black silk dress. I'd brushed them aside. As I did, his eyes raked me from head-to-toe.

"I didn't expect to see you here. You look lovely, Isla."

I look completely out of place. I knew the event was formal. I'd gotten that memo but this is one of three dresses that I always wear to an event like this. It's not elegant by any means. It's simple and understated.

"Thank you," I say quietly. "I should probably go. Someone is waiting for me."

"Wait." His voice is smooth as he tilts his head to the side. "Is that someone Davis Benoit? I saw you talking with him earlier."

I shouldn't be surprised that he knows who Davis is. There was a generous write up of him in the Sunday arts section of the paper last month. It ran in conjunction with the announcement that he'd been offered a position in an artist-in-residency program with one of the most influential cellists in the world.

"That's him," I answer steadily.

"How do you know him?" He glances at a couple standing near us. "Did he come to watch the performance? Are you his date?"

I study his face, wondering if anywhere beneath that impenetrable expression, there's a hint of jealousy. I can't see it. I can't imagine it either. He's so gorgeous and in control. He could approach virtually any woman in this room and have her naked, and on her knees, within five minutes.

"Davis is gay," I shoot back. "We met when I lived in Chicago. We've been friends since."

A small grin flows over his lips. "I was mistaken."

"Apparently." I half-shrug. "How's Cicely?"

"Cicely? Your manager?"

I don't need him to remind me that I answer to her. Tonight is an escape from the boutique. It's a chance for me to be who I really am. I don't want to think about tomorrow when I have to go back to work and face Cicely again.

"Your date," I counter.

He cocks his left brow. "The misunderstandings are mutual, Ms. Lane. I'm here alone."

"Cicely said she had plans with you, I just assumed…" I begin before I catch sight of her approaching from the right. "I assumed you two came together."

He turns his head towards her. "I'm not here with her, or anyone, for that matter. She's one of a group of employees we invited."

I shouldn't care that she's not dating him. It shouldn't matter to me that he's here, in this room, staring at me, but it does.

"I want to apologize for what happened at the boutique." He reaches forward as if he's going to touch my hand, but then he pulls his back. "I didn't have all the facts when Cicely called me. If I had, I never would have questioned you."

"I gave you my word that I wouldn't break the rules. I don't break my word, Mr. Foster."

"Isla, there you are." I feel a hand on my shoulder just as I hear Davis say my name. "It's time. We need to go."

I suck in a deep breath, sorry that this moment has to end. "It was nice to see you, sir. I hope you enjoy your evening."

"I will, Isla." His eyes lock on mine. "I most certainly will."

CHAPTER FOURTEEN

Gabriel

"We need to mingle, Gabriel." My mother pulls on my forearm. "That's what we came here for."

I don't remember what I came here for. All I can remember is the way Isla looked at me when she questioned me about Cicely. There was an invitation woven into her eye's response when I told her I was alone. Her body backed that up when I glanced down to see the outline of her swollen nipples beneath the silk of the dress she's wearing.

She'd walked away from me without a turn back. It only upped my desire for her. She may think she's coy but I felt it. I felt the palpable tension between us.

"There's a string quartet playing in the atrium. I want to see that before we go into the concert hall."

Denying my mother anything at this point is only going to result in a temper tantrum to rival a child's. I came here to further the profile of Foster Enterprises so I'm committed to doing that even if my body is craving a taste of Isla.

"You go ahead." I gesture towards the entrance to the atrium. "I need a drink."

"Fine." My mother runs her finger along my chin. "I don't like this bristle, by the way. You need to shave that."

I nod. I'll allow her to continue to think that her opinion weighs heavily on me. It doesn't anymore. My mother's influence is restricted to a constant reminder of the type of woman I don't want to become involved with.

I love my mother endlessly but her insecurities are exhausting. I've been witness to her self-doubt and the consequences of that my entire life.

I hesitate as I approach one of the servers, knowing that I should be in the midst of the crowd, shaking hands and talking about the good work the charity I'm here to support is doing. I curse under my breath, adjust the arm of my jacket and walk towards the atrium, hoping at some point, I'll see Isla again before the night is over.

***

She's more beautiful now than when I saw her in the lobby. She's different in this space, with her eyes closed, and her body moving slowly to the music.

Her hands are elegant, gifted and as she tilts her chin up at the last note, I realize that this isn't something I'd ever imagined when she stood in my office begging for a second chance to sell lingerie at my boutique or when I saw her at Skyn, using her body to capture the attention of every man in that club.

This young woman has the entire room enthralled. I'd noticed the haunting sounds of the violin the moment I stepped into the space. I'd pushed my way politely through the spellbound crowd until I stood next to my mother mere feet from where the quartet had set up. That's when I saw who was creating the lingering melody that hung in the air. It's Isla.

She parts her lips as soft applause fills the space. I join in, tapping my hands together quietly as I stare at her, in awe of what I've just witnessed.

A dark haired woman holding a viola speaks softly to her. Isla nods and touches her shoulder gently before she pulls the bow back and glides it across the strings of the violin resting beneath her chin.

The woman joins in, her viola a perfect accompaniment to the tender sounds of Isla's violin. Davis Benoit is next to her, a cello perched at the ready. Another violinist is playing but I hear nothing, nothing, but the music that Isla is producing.

I look down at my mother who is captivated by the sounds, her eyes closed, her body slowly swaying as she finds comfort in the music.

This is one of the loves of her life. As children, she'd take us to the symphony when our friends were going to blockbuster movies. She enrolled my brothers and me in music lessons, but Caleb and I failed miserably. It was Asher, my youngest brother, who found his passion there.

I know talent when I see it. I've been trained by my mother's ear to recognize a true gift and that's what Isla possesses.

I feel a tap on my shoulder that I try to ignore, instead keeping my eyes focused solely on Isla. She's enchanting and with each new piece of music she plays, I'm more compelled to stand in place.

"Gabriel." A voice punctures the moment, seeping into my ear. "This is important. We need to talk right now."

I recognize the voice instantly. It's a friend of my father's; a man who worked for our company for decades before I stepped in and pushed the old ways, and him, aside. He was dead weight, pulling a hefty salary for essentially traveling on our dime. He did nothing and when I cut him a severance check and sent him on his way, I'd dealt with the wrath of my father. Our relationship has never fully recovered from that but the company has. I've increased our profits each year since then and I see no end in sight for our success.

I ignore him, hoping he'll recognize my inattention as a refusal to speak. He doesn't. He becomes more persistent, tapping me on the back now, his voice raising a full notch.

The woman playing the viola mutters something indistinguishable under her breath but the words, and disdain, are directed at me. I'm not going to tarnish this moment for Isla so I turn quickly on my heel directing him through the crowd and out of the room.

"What the fuck do you want, Cyril?" I don't try and temper my annoyance.

"It's Roman." He looks past me towards the atrium. "Was that Gianna with you?"

"That's none of your business. What about my father?"

I force myself to face him. His ineptitude may have cost him his job but he's still trying to claw his way back into my good graces. I want nothing to do with the man.

"You haven't heard yet?"

His non-answer only irks me more. "If you have something to say do it now so I can focus on my evening."

"Your father is getting married."

"What?" I snap back. "To who?"

"Caterina Omari." He takes a step back as if he's uncertain of how I'll react to that.

She's a model whose name means nothing to me. She'd thrown herself at both Caleb and me when she was in the vying for a spot in the woman's fashion show in Paris two years ago. I'd turned her down swiftly. Caleb, not one to mute his opinion for anyone, had chastised her in the press for being unprofessional. Neither of us had any interest. Apparently my father does.

"He's a grown man. His decisions are his own." I turn back towards the atrium and pause. "Send him my regards."

CHAPTER FIFTEEN

Isla

"Your grandmother would have been so proud of you tonight, Isla." Davis wraps his arm around my shoulder as we exit the concert hall. "I wish she could have been here to see you."

I smile at his gentle words. My grandma's death has been difficult on Davis too. He'd known her since he was a kid first learning to play the cello.

After her retirement, she'd become one of the most beloved private music teachers in Chicago. Her schedule was always full, a smile permanently on her face. Music was her passion and she'd passed that, and many other things, on to me.

"She would have been so proud of you too." I tap his hand. "You are one of her greatest success stories."

"Me?" He takes a step back to nudge his father's elbow. "Did you hear that, dad? Isla is singing my praises again."

I laugh out loud.

"I'm going to miss you like crazy when you go to Israel." I close my eyes, trying to curb my emotions. "Who is going to call me late at night to ask if I've practiced?"

His smile brightens. "I'm going to call you every day and you're going to keep practicing. Not that you need to practice. You were the star of the show tonight, Isla."

"I have nothing on them." I motion towards the main stage. Watching the Philharmonic perform tonight had been our gift for volunteering to be part of the benefit arts' event. Along with a classical guitarist, a pianist and a horn duo, we agreed to participate as a way to showcase young talent.

When Davis got the call asking our quartet to take part, he didn't hesitate to say yes. It's not only an amazing opportunity; it's also our last chance to perform together. The new cellist, a woman slightly older than me, will step into his place late next month when we are booked for a dedication ceremony at city hall.

"You're going to be on that stage one day." Davis looks down at the worn violin case in my hands. "I'll be sitting front and center watching."

"We both will," Mr. Benoit says through a smile. "It's your birthday tomorrow, isn't it, Isla? Let's go for a drink. It's my treat. It's not every day that you turn twenty-one."

I should point out that I'm not going to be twenty-one for another hour and I left my fake ID at home. In fact, I haven't used it since that night at Skyn. I'm still debating whether I'll ever go back there.

"I think I'll just head home." I look back at the now vacant concert hall. I had hoped to see Mr. Foster again but that hasn't happened.

"There's a car for us to use." Davis raises both brows. "It's mainly so I can take my cello back to my hotel."

"Fancy," I drawl. "I have to carry this with me on the bus."

99

"You'll come with us." Davis extends his hand towards me. "We'll drop you on our way."

"That won't be necessary." I hear the unmistakable growl of Gabriel Foster's voice just as his hand touches the small of my back. "I'll be taking Isla home."

***

I look at the back of the seat in front of me yet again. The driver had placed my violin case on the front passenger seat before he held the back door open for me.

"I'm guarding it with my life, Isla." Mr. Foster's smile is soft and inviting. "It's a treasure. I had no idea you played the violin."

I had no idea he'd insist that I accept his offer for a ride home.

At first, I refused, telling him that I wanted to spend time with Davis before he moves, but he'd been charming as he persisted. I'd finally agreed when I saw Davis giving me a thumbs-up behind Mr. Foster's back. He may think that the man has ulterior motives for inviting me into the backseat of his chauffeur driven sedan, but I know better. He's curious about my music. It caught him off guard.

"You're remarkable." He presses a button on a console in front of us that brings up a barrier of privacy glass separating us from the driver. "How long have you played?"

"Forever," I say honestly. "I've been playing most of my life."

"You studied violin?"

"I took music classes," I go on quickly, "general music classes that all kids take in school but it was my grandmother who taught me."

"Your grandmother?" His dark eyes slide over my face. "She's a music teacher?"

I rake my hand through my hair before I scratch my chin. "My grandmother was the most talented violinist in the world. She ended her career in Chicago. She taught music after that until..."

He adjusts himself on the seat, bending his knee so he's facing me. "Is she gone, Isla? You speak as though she's passed away."

I bite my lower lip. I don't have this conversation willingly with anyone. The pain of her death might not be as raw as it was the morning I found her in her bed cold and unmoving, but it's still a loss I'll never get over. "Yes, sir. She died."

"I'm sorry to hear that." He reaches down to touch my hand.

I stare at his hand, marveling in how large it is compared to mine. "Thank you, Mr. Foster. I appreciate that."

"Gabriel." He runs his index finger over the top of my hand. "I'd prefer if you called me Gabriel."

The feeling of his finger tracing a path over my skin gives me goosebumps. The sound of his voice touches me in a way that is both unnerving and arousing. "Gabriel. I'll call you Gabriel."

"I'm the first to admit that I have no musical talent at all. My brother inherited all the talent in our family."

101

"You mean Asher?" I ask without thinking. "Of course you mean Asher. He's everywhere right now."

"He's in Tokyo, right now, on tour." His mouth twitches. "I'm still adjusting to my youngest brother being a rock star."

"I think he's incredibly talented," I offer. "I love his music. I listen to it all the time."

He slides one of his hands over the seat back behind my head, the other jumps to the black leather on the seat next to me caging me in. He's so close that I can smell the scent of his cologne. "Tell me about your birthday, Isla. I heard your friends mention it tonight. What does a woman like you have planned for such a special day?"

I peer out the tinted window at the streets of Manhattan. It's near midnight but the city is still alive. People are walking along the sidewalks, taxis and cars are speeding past us as we drive towards my apartment. "I haven't thought about it."

"There must be something special you'd enjoy? Perhaps an experience you've never had before."

I turn quickly to look at him.

"A woman your age should be experiencing new things." His hand leaves the seat; trailing a slow path up my arm towards my shoulder before it reaches my chin. "The city is filled with many possibilities."

I feel a flush of desire race up my neck. I swallow hard trying to chase away the lump that is there in my throat. Even if I wanted to respond, I doubt that any sound that escapes me right now would resemble anything other than a deep and uncontrollable moan.

The car lurches to a stop but I'm so mesmerized by the way he's looking at me that I don't move an inch. I don't want to. I've never been this close to a man like this and I've definitely never had a man look at me the way he is right now.

"You're home." He leans in closer. "Let me be the first to wish you a happy birthday."

I catch my breath as his head dips towards me. I moan faintly and just as I begin to close my eyes, I feel his lips brush against my cheek.

"Happy Birthday, Isla," he says in a whisper against my skin. "May it be the best year of your life."

CHAPTER SIXTEEN

Gabriel

Her skin smells like perfection. I linger once I've kissed her cheek, knowing that I need to step out of the car so I can walk her into the building.

We're still, so still. Her breathing is ragged and fast. My lips still resting against her, my hands fisted in a visible sign of the internal struggle I'm fighting.

I want her.

I want to kiss her beautiful lips.

I want to fuck her sweet, lush body.

"Mr. Foster." Her voice is so soft that I can barely hear her. "Gabriel, please."

Please.

Her hand moves from her lap to my forearm. She grips the material of my jacket in her fist before she releases it. I tremble as I feel it move up my bicep, my shoulder and then finally, it rests against the back of my neck.

It's an invitation; just as the sound of her breathing is. Just as the movement of her thighs against the leather, as she parts them a touch, is.

Her hand glides higher, stopping as it reaches the base of my hair. Her fingers float along my skin, softly, so softly.

"Please." It's my voice this time. I don't beg. I won't beg.

Fuck it. I will beg for her.

Her hand knots in the bottom of my hair as she arches her neck, slides her lips along my cheek and finally, finally I taste her on my mouth.

I groan into the kiss as her soft lips push into mine. I slide my tongue into her mouth, wanting to savor her in any way I can.

My reward is the sweetest of moans along with the faint sound of her moving on the leather seat of the car.

I tug her into my lap so she's facing me, her thighs straddling mine. I hear my phone ringing in the distance. It's not important. It can't be important. Nothing is as important as this.

She adjusts herself, grinding into my erection through my pants. My chest heaves at the sensation. I've never come just from the stimulation of a woman's body or hands on my cock. It's always taken a greedy mouth or a slick pussy to get me off. I've never orgasmed like this, yet now, I know that I could.

I feel I might if she doesn't stop moving.

"Isla." I run my hands up her thighs, pushing the skirt of her dress higher. "Your skin is so soft."

My phone rings again. This time the brittle bite of it halts her movements.

"It might be important." Her breath touches my lips in the instant before her lips do.

I shake my head gripping her thighs tighter. She pushes her panties into my crotch, circling, baiting, wanting.

"You're a beautiful woman," I whisper as I look down at her thighs. "Every part of you is beautiful."

Her breath hitches as I push the dress even higher, revealing the sheer black panties she's wearing.

"Jesus, Isla." I move my left hand, inching it up her thigh.

A brash knock on the privacy glass startles her so much she leans back almost tumbling from my lap. My hands jump to her waist, pulling her into my chest.

"What?" I bark. "What is it, Charles?"

The glass lowers not more than an inch. "Mr. Foster, I apologize."

My phone rings again. I look down at where it's vibrating in the inner pocket of my jacket. "What's going on, Charles? I assume your interruption is related to these incessant calls."

"It's your mother, sir," he says loudly. His voice tempered by the glass. "She's been taken to the hospital."

***

I step into the Emergency Department and I'm immediately overcome with a sense of impending doom. There are no reporters demanding a statement. I didn't pass one photographer in the lobby trying to gain access to my mother's room.

This is the third time this year that my mother has complained of chest pains. Each of the previous two times, she had on full makeup when she arrived via ambulance. It hadn't taken more than an hour for the doctors to determine that it was anxiety causing her discomfort.

I found out later, much later, that she'd arranged for the press to be there both times. It was sympathy she was looking for. It was a thinly veiled plan to catapult her name back into the spotlight, and my father's view, for a time.

"Ben," I call out my cousin's name as I see him standing next to a nurse. "It's mother. She was brought in."

"Gabriel." He shoves the tablet in his hand at the nurse before he walks towards me. "We've been waiting for you."

I don't hesitate as he hugs me, tightly. We haven't always been close but that's changed since he mended fences with his twin brother, Noah. Ben had pulled away from the family after his mother's death and we lost touch. Now that he's in New York and working as the head of the Emergency Department at one of the city's busiest hospitals, I see him regularly. We've forged a friendship that has been good for us both.

"How is she?" I hear the tremble in my own voice as I pat the side of his cheek. "I tried calling Caleb on the way here but he wasn't answering.
He rests his hand on my back. "We're running tests. Caleb and Rowan are with her. I'll take you to them."

Tests. The word itself doesn't define a thing. She's had tests before and each time the results have been the same. She's anxious. She gets worked up. She demands attention.

"Did anyone call Asher?" Her voice is the first thing I hear when I push the blue curtain separating her cubicle from others aside. "Will he come? Is he coming to see me?"

107

Caleb is sitting in a plastic chair, drawn close to the bed. Rowan, still in the silver sheath dress she wore earlier, is standing behind him, her hands resting on his shoulders.

"He can't right now, Gianna," she says quietly. "I told him we'll call him once we know more."

"I want to speak to him." Her voice quivers. "Can someone get him on the phone?"

I step forward, not only to answer her question, but to relieve my brother from his post. "I'm here. I came when I heard."

Her eyes drift lazily over my face, never stopping to acknowledge my presence. "If you tell Asher I need him, he'll come."

"Tell me how you're feeling, Mother." I pat Caleb on the shoulder signaling for him to move. "I'll sit with you now."

"Her blood pressure spiked." Rowan glances at me. "She was having trouble breathing. I was in the kitchen making her a coffee and Caleb was changing in the bedroom. I heard her fall."

"She went home with you?" I ask with a cock of my brow. My mother has a suite at the hotel the company owns in midtown. It's a private space dedicated just to her for when she's in New York.

Caleb squeezes my shoulder. "I thought it best. I was hoping we could both speak with her in the morning together about the latest development with dad."

I cast my gaze down at the bed. It's obvious that this is more than an anxiety attack. The color has drained completely from her face. She's visibly shaking.

"Are you alright?" I lean down to kiss her forehead. "What happened? Did you feel faint?"

Her bottom lip quivers slightly before her eyes settle on Caleb and then me. "He called when I stepped into the powder room."

I take a deep breath, understanding now. She knows. Father called to tell her.

"I think my heart is broken." Her hand, with a tube attached to administer an IV, rests in the middle of her chest. "He loves someone else. He's never going to love me again."

CHAPTER SEVENTEEN

Isla

"Have you ever been in love, Isla?"

I wonder if this is a trick question. It might be genuine but it's doubtful. I'll answer honestly because that's the best policy, or so they say. Besides, this conversation may actually help to get my mind off of Gabriel. I'm still floating after what happened in his car last night. "No, I've never been in love."

"Is it because of your weight?"

Well, fuck. I stepped right into that.

"What's wrong with my weight?"

Cicely's eyes run over the same pink wrap dress I wear at least once a week. "Nothing. I mean you're not exactly overweight. I guess you're what people refer to as curvy."

I guess you're what I refer to as a raging bitch.

"I haven't had any complaints." I smooth my hands down my sides to my waist.

"You said you have a boyfriend," she segues effortlessly. "Don't you love him?"

"No." I pull more bras out of the cardboard box at my feet. "I had a boyfriend and I didn't love him."

"He dumped you, didn't he?"

Seriously, Cicely? Get over yourself already.

"The break up was mutual," I say even though I know I should walk away from her so this

HAZE   *Deborah Bladon*

conversation, whatever it is, can end. I've been back
here helping her unpack the delivery for more than an
hour. It's Steph's turn to do it now. "What about you,
have you ever been in love?"

"Yes."

The answer catches me so far off guard that I
drop the bras in my hands back into the box. "You've
been in love?"

"Once." She swallows so loudly that I'm sure
everyone in the boutique can hear it. "It was a long
time ago. I was young."

She's still young. "What was he like?"

Her brow furrows slightly as she picks up the
bras and begins sorting them herself. I watch in
silence as she moves her lips, as if she's rehearsing
what she'll say.

"It's your birthday today, isn't it?" She gives
me a weak smile. "I forgot to wish you a happy
birthday this morning."

I've never felt pity for Cicely before. She
presents herself as closed-off and cold. Maybe that's
just a façade and beneath all of that is a heart that has
been tortured and broken. Perhaps she was hurt so
deeply that she can't allow herself to feel anything for
anyone, not even a hint of kindness or compassion.

"Thank you." I smile back.

"You should get back out on the sales floor."
She nods towards the stockroom's open door with her
chin. "The merchandise can't sell itself."

***

"I believe this belongs to you." Gabriel holds my violin case in his hands. "I'm sorry I didn't return it earlier."

I shake my head slightly. "No, please. You have nothing to apologize for. How is your mother?"

He brushes against me to place the case on the front counter. "She'll be fine. It was exhaustion and stress. She'll take a day or two to recover in the hospital. Then we'll go from there."

I glance across the boutique to where Cicely is helping a customer. "I'm glad that she's fine. I was worried after you got that call last night."

He takes a step forward, his hand leaping to the dark blue tie around his neck. He adjusts it as he looks down at me. "If it were anyone else in dire need, I would have told them to go to hell."

I cast my eyes to the floor as I feel a blush race over my cheeks. He'd been a gentleman after the driver had told him about his mother. He slid me off his lap, exited the car almost immediately and then helped me out. After walking me to my building's front door, he'd kissed my forehead before sprinting back to the car. "Thank you for giving me a ride home."

"You can thank me by allowing me to buy you dinner tonight, for your birthday."

I look up and into his eyes. "Tonight? You want to go for dinner tonight?"

Exhaling roughly, he steps even closer. "I realize it's short notice. You have plans, don't you?"

They're not official plans. When I'd walked through the door of the apartment last night, Nigel and Cassia were curled up under a blanket on the sofa. I felt an immediate sense of relief when I saw that they were both clothed. I'd tried to scurry past them to my bedroom but Cassia had stopped me to insist that I have dinner tonight with both her and Nigel. I'd agreed, mainly because I was so tired and still riding the high of kissing Gabriel just minutes before.

"I told my roommate and her boyfriend that I would have dinner with them," I say honestly.

There's a noticeable pause before he says anything and I realize he's waiting for me to continue. He expects that I'll say that I'll change my plans. I can, but Cassia has been so good to me since I moved to New York and the excitement in her smile when I said I'd love to have dinner with them was touching.

"Another time then." He steps back.

"I'd like that," I say. "Again, thank you for bringing my violin to me."

"Enjoy your birthday, Isla." He studies my face before his eyes trail down to my dress. "You're on the cusp of an incredible future. I feel honored that I saw you play last night."

The words mean much more than he'll ever know. "Thank you, Gabriel."
A ghost of a grin floats over his mouth. "You listened. I like that. I'll be in touch."

"I'll look forward to it." I take a deep, shaky breath as I watch him turn on his heel and walk out of the store.

This time I know, beyond a shadow of a doubt, that Gabriel Foster was not only checking me out, he's as interested in me as I am in him. This may be the best birthday I've ever had.

CHAPTER EIGHTEEN

Gabriel

It was mid-afternoon when the floral bouquet I'd ordered for Isla was delivered. I'd been insistent with the florist about the flowers she included. I don't have any knowledge about what Isla prefers but I know what I find beautiful. I wanted something fragrant and bright that will bring a smile to her gorgeous face.

It had.

She'd called my office shortly after three, asking to speak to me. I was in a meeting but Sophia had been instructed to interrupt me the moment Ms. Lane called.

Her voice is as soft on the phone as it is when I speak to her in person. I could hear the sincere gratitude in her tone.

The card, delivered with the bouquet, was a request for a celebratory drink at my favorite bar after her dinner plans. She'd agreed on the phone to meet me there at eleven.

Six hours from now.

It's a risk, perhaps not even a calculated one. The moment we kissed last night, I was lost to it all. To the need to know her, the hunger to be near her, and the constant and always present desire to fuck her.

"Are you going to make time for mom today, or not?" Caleb rounds the corner and walks through the open doors of my office. "I was just at the hospital and she said you're a no show."

Naturally she'd say that. I stopped by there after I'd been to the boutique to return Isla's violin. My mother had been upright, sitting in a chair by the window, chatting away on her smartphone to someone who obviously sympathized with her plight.

I'd sat on the edge of her hospital bed, for a full twenty minutes, waiting for her to end the call, but she hadn't. My day was too busy to devote it to listening to my mother discuss what nail polish color would be the best choice since her manicurist was on her way to the hospital.

After a quick kiss on her forehead, and a chat with my cousin, Ben, about the improvement in her condition, I'd left.

"I was there earlier." I swipe my finger across my tablet. "She was talking on the phone."

"She's waiting for you to visit her." He ignores everything I just said. "Rowan is stopping by the hospital after work. You can catch a ride with her."

"I have plans." I do. I'm going to the gym before I take a long, hot shower. After that, I'll get dressed and then head to the bar to meet Isla.

He arches his left brow. "She's going to be pissed."

"I'll call her to say goodnight." I gesture towards my phone. "She'll get over it, Caleb. She always does."

***

I'm on my second scotch when I see her walk into the bar. Her hands are holding the skirt of her short black dress in place against the harsh wind that blew up late this evening. Her hair, likely polished and pristine when she left her apartment for dinner, is now a tangled mess around her face.

She looks disheveled in the most alluring way possible.

Her eyes scan the dimly lit space just as I stand. I see the instant recognition and perhaps, relief, in her expression when her hand rises in a small wave.

She walks towards me. Steady and determined in her heels. Although they give her a fair few inches in height, I still tower over her.

"Gabriel." Her tongue darts out to wet her bottom lip. "I'm sorry if I'm late."

She's not late. I'd paced the floor of my penthouse for a solid hour before I called for my driver to bring me here. That was shortly after nine.

I've been sitting in this chair, tending to emails on my phone, while waiting. I shared the table briefly with a designer we'd done business with three years ago and then twice with women who took it upon themselves to join me.

I'd made it clear, quickly, that I was saving my time, and attention, for someone else.

Any other night, I might have bought one, or both, a drink. I'd listen to them tell me about their lives and the shortcomings with the men they've been with before. Then, I'd pay the tab, escort them to a hotel and within minutes, I'd be fucking every last ounce of stress in my body away.

Not tonight. Tonight is only for Isla.

"You're not late." I grab her upper arms as I lean in to kiss her cheek. "You look beautiful tonight."

The pressure of my grip brings a small moan to the surface. Her lips part as she looks up and into my face. "You look nice too."

Compliments, like that, are part of my life. I accept them, gratefully, but I never absorb them. New York City is filled with handsome, successful men. I know that.

Hearing the words from Isla is different. It's understandable since she's incredibly different.

"How was your dinner?" I ask as I pull on the back of a chair next to where I was seated.

She lowers herself into it with a nod of her head in appreciation. "It was delicious. They took me to a restaurant in Greenwich Village. It was so good."

I sit down again, but not before moving my chair closer to her. "What was the name of the place?"

Her eyes slide over my thighs before she looks up and at me." I'm not sure. We all went together in a taxi. I have pictures of my dinner though."

She reaches to where she'd placed her clutch on the table. The motion pulls the front of her dress taut, the fullness of her breasts visible beyond the low cut neckline.

I take a drink. I may need another.

"It was really good." She scrolls through the images on her phone. I catch glimpses of her next to a dark haired woman her age, a pigeon eating breadcrumbs from a sidewalk and then, a plate of pasta.

She pushes the phone towards me. "I took a few. You can see what I mean. It tastes as divine it looks."

Her exuberance is contagious. I can't help but smile when I watch her speak.

I drop my eyes from her face to her phone, resting on the table in front of me. I stare at the screen and the bowl of pasta she deemed worthy enough to capture it in a badly lit photograph.

"There are two more pictures." She leans closer, her hand brushing against mine. "Just swipe."

I do as told, running my finger over the screen.

"That's not it." She reaches forward to grab the phone but I'm too quick. I scoop her hand in mine to stop it.

I dip my chin towards the screen and the image of Isla in a blue dress. It's obvious she took the picture in a mirror. "This is one of our designs. You look stunning in this, Isla."

Her lips move slightly as her eyes search mine. "I just wanted to try it on. I went to Arilia one day before work."

"I had no idea the dress could look like this." I pick up the phone, tilting it slightly to the left to gain more light from the overhead fixture. "You belong in this dress."

She reaches forward to gently take the phone from my grasp. "The dresses in the Arilia store are all beautiful. The designers are really talented."

I don't press the issue when I see the server approaching. I wait as he asks her what she'd like to drink.

She smooths her hand over her hair, pushing the soft blond locks behind her left ear. "I think I should stick to a sparkling water. I'm trying to avoid alcohol right now."

"You are?" I ask with a grin. "This is your twenty-first birthday. You don't want a drink to celebrate?"

"No," she says assuredly. "I can't. I promised myself I wouldn't drink tonight. I want to remember every moment of my first birthday in Manhattan. Sometimes when I drink things get foggy."

I glance down at my watch. "There are still forty-five minutes of your birthday left. I'd like to make those memorable. "

Her lips curve. "What do have in mind?"

I pull myself up from the chair as I stand and extend my hand towards her. "Come with me, Isla. I'll make this a day you'll never forget."

CHAPTER NINETEEN

Isla

"You wouldn't stand close to the edge." I tap his chest lightly. "Does the world know that Gabriel Foster is scared of heights?"

He laughs deeply, the sound bouncing against the steel walls of the elevator. "I'm not scared of heights, Isla. I was watching you enjoy the view."

"Is that your story?" I giggle. "I can play along for the press if they ask."

His brows shoot up. "You would do that for me, Ms. Lane? You won't tell the media hounds that I took you up to the roof of the Foster Enterprises building so you could see the stars while I stood far away from the edge, trembling in my boots?"

"They're not boots." I point to his feet. "They're fancy Foster shoes."

"Fancy Foster shoes?" His hand jumps to my chin before he runs his fingertip over my bottom lip. "That just may be the hashtag we use on social media when we launch the new men's shoe collection."

I part my lips slightly, pushing my tongue out so it can touch his finger. "You're not in charge of marketing are you? If you are, you shouldn't be."

Tipping his chin, his eyes rake me slowly from head-to-toe just as the elevator chimes its arrival on the top floor. "You're certain you want to join me for a bottle of sparkling water?"

"Yes, sir, I'm sure."

His gaze meets mine and I see something shift. The playful parts of him have slipped into the background again. The intensity that is almost always there is present now.

The doors of the lift open. His head turns slightly towards the expansive space, complete with large windows that give an unobstructed view of the city. "I did promise to make this a day you'll never forget, Isla. Come with me."

***

The entire time that Gabriel and I were on the roof of the Foster Enterprises building I was completely aware of the way he was looking at me. Even when I was near the edge and he was ten feet behind me, I could feel his eyes trained on my back.

I was hoping, when we got into the car, that he'd kiss me again. I wanted that but instead he'd pulled my hand onto his thigh and covered it with his own while he talked about all the things he loved about Manhattan.

Gabriel Foster radiates confidence. He garners attention when he passes people on the street. I saw it for myself when we walked out of the building towards where Charles had parked the car. Several people turned just to look at him. He's handsome in a way that makes you wonder what it's like to kiss him, or touch him. I know now what both of those things feel like and as we sat in the car and I listened to him telling me about the brownstone he grew up in, I saw a flash of something vulnerable in his eyes. He turned quickly to look out at the slow moving traffic but it was there.

I see it again now as he turns towards where I'm standing near the bank of windows that overlook lower Manhattan. "I have something for you, Isla."

It's not what I imagined when he asked if I wanted to join him to cap off the night with a bottle of sparkling water. My lust filled mind thought he'd push me hard against the wall of the elevator, before he kissed me so deeply that my toes curled within the shoes I'm wearing. Then I pictured his hands falling to the hem of my dress before he pulled it over my head in one fluid swoop so he could ravish me.

The something he has for me clearly isn't rock hard and hidden beneath the cover of his expensive pants. It's in the envelope he picked up from a long counter after he poured us each a glass of water.

"What is it?" I ask cautiously.

He tucks the envelope under his arm as he scoops the two glasses of water in his palms. I watch in silence as he walks towards me. He'd slid his suit jacket off once we entered the apartment before he'd loosened his tie. It's only a slight adjustment but it changes him. His hair had caught the wind when we'd stood on the roof and even though he'd raked his hand through it in the elevator, it did nothing to tame it. He looks different now than every other time I've seen him. He's softer, less in control.

I take the glass of water when he offers it, downing half of it. He watches me carefully before he pulls the glass away from me and sets it next to his on a large steel coffee table.

"Open it." He pushes the envelope in my hand.

I stare down at it.

Ms. Lane.

That's all that's written on it. The ink is black; the handwriting masculine. It's obvious he wrote this and not the card that arrived with the elaborate floral bouquet that was delivered to the boutique this afternoon. As desperate as I was to shield the card from Cicely, she had caught sight of it over my shoulder. Her bitchy attitude for the remainder of my shift was evidence of that.

I look up and into his dark eyes before I drop my gaze back to the envelope. I flip it over in my hands, pulling my fingernail across the seal.

The card slides out easily. It's breathtaking. The artwork on the front as striking as anything you'd see displayed in a museum. The colors are vibrant and the design captivating. I scan it, my eyes resting on the unmistakable signature scrawled across the bottom corner.

"This is beautiful," I begin before I pull my gaze up to his face. "This is a Brighton Beck print, isn't it?"

His right brow cocks with the subtle movement of his head as he tilts it ever so slightly. "You're familiar with Brighton Beck's work?"

I run my fingers across my chin. "Yes. This is a print of Voyage. He painted this after the birth of his son. He donated it to a children's hospital in Paris, I think. They sell cards of the prints in the gift shop there to raise money for equipment."

He studies my face, his expression unreadable. I should tell him that I know all of this because my grandmother loved Brighton Beck with a passion that was only matched by her adoration for her music and her thirst for literature. When she bought one of his watercolor paintings at an auction, she'd been giddy. She had it hung over the worn leather chair in the library of her house. Each time I walked in there to talk to her, I'd catch her staring at it. I've followed his career since her death.

"Can I open the card?" I ask tentatively, wanting to break the silence.

"Please," he says as he motions towards my hands with his chin.

I smile softly before I cast my eyes back down to the card and the surprise that waits inside.

CHAPTER TWENTY

Gabriel

Compared to the notable relationships I've had in my life, I don't even know Isla Lane yet. We've spent no more than a few hours together in total. She's years younger than I am. She has an entry level position at one of the many boutiques my company owns. She was honest on her employment application when she mentioned that her community college career was limited to just a year. She was in pursuit of a Bachelor of Music degree but apparently she's put that on hold.

I earned dual degrees at Princeton. I know many of the world's most influential people on a first name basis. I own several apartments on different continents and I covet art because I find it captivating in a way that many people don't.

Yet, now, as I watch Isla staring at the greeting card I purchased months ago I'm in awe. I'd walked into the gift shop of the hospital in Paris after I'd visited one of our executives. She was there, with her husband, standing watch over their newborn daughter who had a simple procedure.

The cards had caught my eye immediately. I'm not a friend of Brighton Beck's but we share common acquaintances and the experience of walking through the corridors of that facility, on my way towards the exit, had been humbling. I've always had my health and to see children struggling with theirs

125

had been enough to prompt me to purchase all the cards they had in stock.

I'd shoved them into a cabinet in my office when I returned to New York but today, thinking of Isla's birthday, I wanted to give her one.

The extent of my gift giving is typically delegated to my assistant, but with Isla I wanted something more. I wanted it be personal. I wanted her face to light up when she saw the card even if I thought her reaction would be restricted to a comment about the beauty of the design.

How the hell could I have known that she'd not only recognize Brighton Beck's work but that she'd understand and appreciate the meaning in the print?

"These are symphony tickets." She cradles the two tickets in her fingers. "These are close to the stage. They're orchestra tickets, aren't they?"

The smile on her face is genuine. It's what I anticipated when I called the box office and tossed out a few well-respected names with the hope of securing two tickets to the sold out performance next week. "I know that your seat last night was in the third balcony. I wanted you to have the experience of being close to the stage."

"My seat was practically outside the building," she says under her breath. "This is amazing."

"You can take whoever you'd like." I brush my fingertips over her hand. "Perhaps Davis Benoit would like to go with you or your roommate."

Her face softens as she looks up at me. Her lips part slightly before she closes them again, her

126

eyes falling back to her hands. "This is a generous gift. Thank you."

"You belong at every performance," I say as I reach down to grab the glass of water I'd poured earlier. "You actually belong on the stage."

She doesn't break my gaze as she absorbs the compliment. I know instinctively that's because she believes there's as much truth in my words as I do. I swallow the water in one long gulp, all the while regretting not pouring myself something stronger.

"Will you go with me?"

It's the invitation I had hoped she'd offer. I could have easily invited her to the performance straightaway but I wanted her to choose. I want her to crave my presence next to her, just as much as I crave hers.

I set the glass on the table before I take a measured step closer to her. "I'd be honored to go with you, Isla. A late dinner after the performance would make for a perfect evening."

"A late dinner here?" Her eyes scan the dimly lit room before they settle on the view of the city.

I lessen the space between us again as I move even closer to her. The distance separating us now is little more than mere inches. "I can arrange that. Is that what you want? To come back here after we watch the performance?"

She places the card and envelope on the table before she turns so her back is against the window. Her heels shift slightly, ever so slightly, as she laces her fingers together in front of her. "Yes, I want that."

I stare at her face, entranced with how utterly beautiful she is. Her nose is delicate, her lips full and pink. Her blue eyes are wide and framed by long lashes. She's breathtaking, even though her lipstick has smudged slightly and her hair is even more tousled than it was earlier.

I slowly unclasp the cuff link on my left wrist, sliding it into the pocket of my pants before I roll the sleeve of my white dress shirt to the elbow. Her eyes watch my every movement as I do the same with my right arm.

"Has it been a birthday to remember?" My hand darts to the sash around her waist. "Will you remember this day?"

Her eyes are fastened on my fingers. I pull on the sash softly. It offers little resistance before it gives and releases into my hand.

"I think I'll remember it always, sir."

I step forward, my hands leaping to her neck, cradling her face in my palms. I float the pad of my thumb over her lower lip. I lean down to kiss her softly, tasting the sweetness of her breath. "I'm going to make certain you never forget it."

CHAPTER TWENTY-ONE

Isla

Enjoy, Gabriel.

They're just two words. They were all he'd written in the card he'd given to me. He might have known the literal meaning they'd hold. He couldn't have known what it would feel like when he lowered his face to mine and kissed me. I'd melted. I'd held fast to his hands as they cupped my cheeks when he licked his tongue over my bottom lip and I'd moaned, so loud, when his hand dropped to my thigh.

"You're so perfect." His lips trace a path along my cheek. "I've thought about this for days."

I want to say something in return; something poetic and thoughtful so that his memory will cling to this night just as long as mine will. I doubt that's possible.

I will never forget the scent of his skin as he bows his head to brush his lips across my neck. I will never forget the softness of his hair as I wrap my fingers through it and I'm never going to forget how it will feel to come beneath his touch.

He pulls back just enough that it tugs a whimper from somewhere deep within me. My hand darts to my mouth, my cheeks flushing instantly with the knowledge that my body is responding to him on a basic, primal level.

"You're going to think I say this…" he stops himself mid-thought to lean forward to kiss me softly.

129

"You looked so beautiful when you walked into the bar tonight, Isla. I've never wanted to touch a woman more."

The words push me back on my feet but his arms circle me, holding me in place.

"You want me," I say breathlessly, realizing that it sounds more like a question than a statement.

His lips press hard against mine in response. I push my body into his, wanting to lessen the distance. My hands jump to his chest, my fingers fumbling aimlessly for the buttons.

"No," he whispers the word into our kiss. "Turn around."

I ignore his words. In my desperation to feel his skin touching mine, I grab hold of his tie, pulling at it, trying to wrench the knot free.

His hands are on mine before I have time to think. He bites my bottom lip, his tongue immediately tracing a path over the spot to soothe it.

I step back, not just from the sudden burst of pain but from the action. My fingers jump to my lip, instinctively covering what I know will be a swollen bruise.

"That hurt," I say softly. "You hurt me."

He steadies his stance as he cradles my chin in his hand tilting my head back so our eyes meet. It's then that he leans forward, his breath a soft whisper against my ear. "That's a prelude of what's to come, Isla. Tell me if you want me to stop. Just say the word."

I take a half step back wanting the distance to catch my breath as much as to look in his eyes. "Haze."

130

"Haze?" His brow furrows. "What is haze?"

I felt it the moment I saw him in the boutique. That feeling only intensified when I was alone with him in his office and he stood next to me. When I was in his lap in the car, he wanted me. His body couldn't hide his desire. It was there in the way he touched my thighs. I could sense it in his kiss. He's offering exactly what I want.

I exhale softly as I look up and into his eyes. "Haze is my safeword. If it's too much and I want you to stop, I'll say it."

The growl that emanates from him almost drives me to my knees. It pushes him to his and as he turns me towards the glass, hikes my dress up to my hips, and slowly pulls my panties off, I know that my life will never be the same again.

***

"Brace yourself," he says in a deep, firm tone; his voice the only sound in the room.

I lean my cheek into the cool glass of the window. I can feel his breath on my tender flesh. I've felt exposed with lovers before but it's never been like this. I'm standing in my heels, my pussy on ripe display with his mouth and tongue so close. He's so close I can feel every movement of his lips when he speaks.

"You're beautiful, Isla." His tongue slowly grazes my smooth folds. "You're so wet. You've been wet all night, haven't you?"

"I've been wet since you walked into the boutique weeks ago."

131

I feel quick movement behind me as he rises to his feet and pulls down the zipper at the back of my dress before he yanks it over my head and tosses it on the floor. "You wanted me then? It was the day you propositioned me."

I nod my head as a meek, "yes," falls from my lips. I push back, feeling his rock hard cock pressing into my ass through the fabric of his pants.

"Tell me what you were going to do." His fingers trace a path around my bare nipples before he pinches first the right, and then the left, hard.

"Ah, please." I rub my thighs together, my right hand dropping from the glass to my pussy.

His shoes kick at my feet, forcing them farther apart as his hand grabs my wrist, pushing it back to the window. "Keep your hands on the glass or I'll tie them behind your back."

I move them both quickly towards my thighs.

He reacts instantly. His hands find mine, pulling them back up. "Don't do that. I mean it."

"I want it. I want you to tie me up."

"Christ," he mutters into my neck as he grinds himself into me. "This is too much. You're too much."

My cheeks heat as I feel his body pressed against mine. I lean forward, resting my forehead against the glass.

"Tell me," he hisses. "Tell me what you were going to do that first day. If you came to my office tell me what would have happened."

I turn my head to the left to catch sight of his face. The sweat on his upper lip matches the want in his eyes. He's as lost to this as I am.

"I'll show you," I offer with a raise of my brow. "I want to show you."

His eyes close briefly as he swallows hard. "No, not tonight."

"Please," I whine, wanting to show him.

I may not have had a set plan that day in Liore when I offered to show up at his office, but I do now. I want to taste him. I want to slide his cock between my lips so I can hear the sounds he makes when he's chasing his release. I want to give that to him. I want to please him more than I've ever wanted to please any man before.

"I need this." His hand snakes between my legs to cup my pussy. "I want this tonight."

I moan as I grind myself into his fingers.

"Don't move, Isla. Keep your hands on this glass."

I nod faintly before the room falls silent. The only sound is my labored breathing and a soft rustling behind me.

CHAPTER TWENTY-TWO

Gabriel

I eat her with a ferocity I've never felt before. I can't get enough. I lick her, suck her, breathe her scent into me; the taste both intoxicating and addictive. The sounds she makes the most arousing I've ever heard.

Her right hand drops from the glass and into my hair. She tugs on the strands, urging me closer as she grinds herself back onto my face. The bite of pain spurring me on more because I know she'll pay for that. I'll teach her that the pain I desire, and need, is hers.

I slow, licking her pretty pink cunt with soft strokes, wanting to keep her on the edge longer. She's frustrated. I hear it in the soft moans and whimpers. I feel it in her fingers, the way they're clutching, and pulling. She wants to control this. She wants me to give her exactly what she needs.

I pull back and a deep groan escapes her. My cock aches with the sound.

I stand, resting my lips against her cheek. Her hair is a tangled mess, her lips moist and plump. Her skin is glowing with a sheer mist, the product of her writhing against my tongue.

"Gabriel, please," she whines.

"You moved your hand," I lean into her and whisper harshly, my hand gliding across her ass cheek.

She moans beneath my touch, inching herself up to her tiptoes in an effort to line up her dripping wet pussy with my fingers. She's close. I could feel it with my tongue when I circled her swollen clit over and over.

"I want to come," she purrs. "Let me get myself off. I want to touch myself."

I raise my hand in the air before I bring it down to her ass. The sharp crack of my skin on hers fills the room, along with a guttural groan from her lips.

"Again, please?"

Fuck. The request almost drives me back down to my knees.

I run my fingers over her folds, pulling the wetness along her ass, before I slap it again, harder this time.

"Ah, yes. Yes."

I unbuckle my belt, the pressure within too much. I pull down the zipper of my pants, slowly as I watch her ass sway, her hand inching its way back to her core.

I reach down to pick up the sash from her dress. I hold it taut in my fists in front of me. "I said no, beautiful Isla."

I move quickly pulling both her wrists into my hands. I wrap the sash around one and she moves the other into place. Her hands work with me as I bind them together behind her back. She flips them, twists them right along with my movements as if we're in an intricate dance.

"Will you fuck me now?" The words sound foreign as they fall from her sweet lips. "I want to be fucked hard."

Christ, please. Yes.

I look at her face, her right cheek still pressed against the glass. I lean forward, running my fingers along her back before I cradle her chin, moving it just a touch so I can slide my mouth over hers.

The kiss is deep, lush and as soon as I pull away, I'm behind her.

I glide my fingers across her pussy. She's wet, so incredibly wet.

Her breathing quickens. Her ass moves as she slides her feet even farther apart. I stare at her reflection in the glass. Her beautiful eyes are closed. Her lips quivering as she exhales loudly.

My hand grazes the front of my pants. I should do this. It's what I'd planned when I dressed for tonight and slid two condom packages in the pocket of my slacks. I wasn't even sure I'd be able to resist the temptation to be inside of her before we stepped foot off the elevator.

I'd wanted her desperately in the car. My mind conjuring up detailed images of her nude on my lap, riding my dick as we drove through the streets of the city.

I've thought about fucking her since I first saw her.

Her body is everything I imagined and more.

She's literally begging me for it.

All I have to do is sheath my cock and slide it into her wet cunt. I can take her hard against this window. I can claim her right now.

I suck in a deep breath as my hands dart to the glass on either side of her, trapping her there, against me.

"Gabriel." Her voice is barely audible. "Please fuck me."

I rest my forehead against her back aligning my eyes with her bound wrists and beyond that, the curve of her naked ass. I brush my lips across her shoulder, nestling my cheek into the softness of her fragrant skin.

"Haze," I mouth the word silently before I lower myself back to my knees, inhale the sweet scent of her arousal and tongue her pussy until she comes screaming my name.

CHAPTER TWENTY-THREE

Isla

I hear the unmistakable sound of my smartphone's ringtone as it jars me awake. I get that some people are annoyed by those of us who choose music to alert us to a new call, as opposed to those boring old chimes and buzzers.

My ring tone happens to be one of my most favorite things in life and since it's my phone, it's actually no one else's business.

I rub my hand over my face trying to stir the sleep from my eyes. It takes me all of a half second when I open my eyes to realize that this is not my bedroom. This is actually at least four times the size of my bedroom and when I'm at home, I never, ever sleep completely in the nude like I am right now.

"You're awake."

I also never hear a voice like that in my bedroom unless I'm touching myself while I'm thinking about Gabriel Foster.

Gabriel Foster. Did he eat me out over and over again last night or was that a dream?

I sit up and turn sharply to my left just as my phone falls silent.

"You have excellent taste in ringtones, Isla." His voice is deep and has that growl to it that is distinctive. "Bach, is it?"

"No." I shake my head trying to release myself from this dream. "It's not Bach. It's Vivaldi.

You can hear the vulnerability in the notes. That's why I love it so much."

What? What the fuck am I doing right now? My tits are on full display and I'm in a strange bed going over the finer points of my favorite composition.

"You slept soundly." He steps right into my line of sight. "It's near seven now. I'll need to leave for a meeting soon."

I adjust the soft white sheet that is covering me so it shields my breasts from not only his gaze, but the chill in the room. He's dressed in a different suit than he was last night. That one was dark blue. This one is grey. He's shaved, showered and looks ready to take on his day.

My eyes fall to the bed as memories of what happened last night flood me. He'd licked me near the window until I came. Then he'd turned me around. He'd kissed me softly before he untied my wrists, and carried me to his bed. After he brought me to another orgasm with his mouth, he'd gotten on the bed next to me, his face hovering above mine while he ran his index finger over my lips. I'd stared into his eyes until I must have drifted off to sleep.

I had begged him to fuck me in the other room. I'd wanted it so much that any sense of self composure I had disappeared in direct relation to my rising need to feel his cock inside of me.

I heard the sound of his belt loosening and his zipper being drawn down but it stopped there.

He had stalled when I whimpered about wanting his cock and as he fell to his knees to lick me again, I'd felt a rush of embarrassment wash over me.

It's happened before.

139

This isn't the first time I've told a man I like to be tied up only to have him give in to that before conveniently losing my number.

I should apologize for being so wanting. No, I should get my ass out of his bed so I can get to the boutique. I don't have to do anything beyond looking at the undisturbed pillow next to me to know that he didn't sleep in this bed with me.

He owns Foster Enterprises. The company revolves around his schedule. His rush to leave to get to a meeting is nothing more than a polite *'fuck you, Isla,'* and no, not in a good, or satisfying, way.

"The door will lock automatically behind you." He casts his eyes down at the watch on his wrist. "I've left the number for my driver, Charles, on a card by your purse. Call him when you're ready to leave and he'll come up to escort you down to the car."

"I'll do that," I say quietly. "I'll need to leave soon. I have to be at work at nine."

He lowers himself to the edge of the bed so when he sits, he's facing me directly. "I enjoyed last night. You're a remarkable young woman."

Thanks? Is that what I'm supposed to say now?

"I'm running late." He leans forward to brush his lips across my forehead. "I apologize for leaving but it's an important matter."

I nod as he stands, pivots on his heel and walks out of the bedroom. It doesn't matter if it's important or not. The only thing that matters is that I lost all respect for myself when I walked into this apartment last night.

***

"Can I help you?" I grip the towel closer to my body.

The woman who sauntered into the washroom while I was mid shower shakes her head faintly from side-to-side before she turns back to her task at hand which apparently involves replacing Mr. Foster's toothbrush in a glass. She pulls a new, wrapped one from her pocket before she throws the used one in the trash.

"Why are you here?" I can hear the panic in my own voice even though I know she's likely here to clean his apartment. That makes sense save for the uniform and name tag she's wearing.

Her eyes lock on mine in the reflection of the large mirror above the sink. "I'm cleaning. He likes it clean when he leaves."

I knew I should have gone straight home after he left. It was my intention until I stepped into the washroom and saw the spacious marble shower. I felt an uncontrollable desire to wash last night off of my body and out of my mind. I'd tied my hair up with an elastic band I kept in my purse and then just as the hot water hit my back, I'd heard the door of the washroom open.

For a split second my heart stalled, believing it was Gabriel coming back to apologize for… for not fucking me? For rejecting me? For whatever it is that is making me feel so humiliated right now.

It didn't matter though. It was this, quiet, demure and adorable woman who didn't bat one single eyelash when I stepped out of the shower completely stark naked before she handed me a towel.

"Can you come back later?" I plead with her. "I'd like to get ready before I leave."

"He sometimes comes back at a lunch with… he has meetings here at lunch sometimes, sometimes earlier than that." She nods towards the other room. "He likes it cleaned before that. I have to do it now."

Christ, he's a hard ass. He doesn't cut this woman a break.

She won't even give me ten minutes to pull myself together for fear that he'll come back home before she's had a chance to rearrange his toiletries. Wait. Those bottles of shampoo and moisturizer she's replenishing are small. They're so small.

I bolt out of the washroom with the towel still wrapped haphazardly around me. I walk through the attached bedroom and back into the large living room. My eyes scan the area, taking in everything I didn't see last night when the lights were dim and my interest was focused solely on Gabriel.

I turn to the left in search of the other rooms. I walk down a hallway but all that I find is a closed door that leads to a compact washer and dryer.

I march back through the main room, right past the woman who is now dusting the counter. I spot my purse there, with the birthday card and envelope sitting atop it. The hallway at the opposite end of the room leads to a small alcove with a television and an armchair.

"Where's the kitchen?" I ask without thinking, a knot forming in my stomach. "Where is Mr. Foster's kitchen?"

  She half-shrugs without looking up at me. "This suite doesn't have a kitchen. Mr. Foster doesn't eat here. I mean he doesn't cook here."

  I swear I hear her giggle under her breath. That steals every chance I may have had to ask her the obvious question. I can already imagine her reaction.

  I turn back towards the bedroom, slamming the heavy door behind me. I drop the towel as I head straight for the closet. I push both of the doors aside to reveal two white dress shirts, one suit and a single pair of black shoes.

  I pull in a deep breath as I approach a chest of drawers. I tug on the first drawer but it doesn't budge. I'm met with the same resistance when I try to open the second drawer. It's locked. I try them all, knowing as I yank on each that I'll be offered the same result.

  I turn then, my eye catching on the phone atop the night stand. I walk slowly towards it, studying the various labeled buttons. I pick up the receiver and press '0'.

  "Good morning, Mr. Foster."

  "This isn't Mr. Foster," I whisper into the air. "I'm not Mr. Foster."

  "Of course." The woman on the other end of the call is cheery, too cheery for so early in the morning. "Are you ordering breakfast for the two of you? I'll have room service send up his usual. What would you like?"

  I stand silently as I slide open the drawer of the night stand. I don't feel anything as my eyes scan the boxes of condoms and tubes of lubricant, that are next to a pad of paper and a pen, both bearing a hotel's logo.

It now makes total sense why we pulled up to the back of the building last night and entered through a private door before stepping into the elevator. I didn't see anyone. I wasn't paying close enough attention to realize where I was.

"Miss, are you still there?" The voice on the phone startles me. "What can I get you?"

"My pride. I'd like to have my pride back," I whisper into my hand as I cover the mouthpiece before I hang up.

My wish came true. I wanted my birthday to be memorable. I'm pretty sure that I'll never forget that I spent my twenty-first birthday in Gabriel Foster's fuck pad, or in my case, non-fuck pad.

CHAPTER TWENTY-FOUR

Gabriel

"You know this is complete bullshit, Gabriel," Caleb hisses the words out as he slams both his fists onto my desk. "Why the fuck are you doing this?"

I've asked myself the same question repeatedly since I walked out of the hotel suite and into the elevator, leaving Isla behind. The only difference is that Caleb's focused solely on business right now, and I can't get the image of Isla, freshly woken, out of my mind.

"I'm doing this for your mother," I push the words out with a dart of my index finger towards him. "This is for our mother so she doesn't get her name dragged through the press again. Do you honestly think she can handle that right now, Caleb?"

"It's blackmail." He rakes both of his hands through his dark hair. "He's blackmailing us and you're giving in. What the hell has happened to you?"

I've become our mother's keeper. I've been delegated to cleaning up one mess after another while she wanders through her life causing nothing but havoc. He's right about it being bullshit.

When one of the company's attorney's had called me shortly after six this morning, I'd taken the call instantly. I was sitting on a chair near the bed, still fully clothed from last night, as I watched Isla sleep.

I'd held her in my arms after I'd carried her into the bedroom. I'd spread her legs and tongued her sweet cunt to an intense orgasm. She'd moved beneath me on the bed, her hands clutching the linens, pulling on them as her moans filled the air. It took every ounce of strength I had within me not to lower my head again to take her right back to that place. I could listen to her come over and over again and I'd never get enough.

She'd had enough though. I could feel it in the way her muscles went limp and hear it as her breathing slowed. I wanted her to sleep. I wanted to hold her against me all night but it was too much. It had all been too much and after I pulled a blanket over her nude body, I'd sat in the chair next to the bed and watched her sleep. Minutes passed, and then hours and when my phone rang, I'd taken the call in the other room.

I'd shaved, taken a shower and dressed all before the soft sounds of a symphony filled the room. It was the ringtone on her phone and after it quieted, she'd explained in a voice still sultry from sleep the name of the composer and the subtle nuances found within the music.

I've never known anyone like her. I'd never tasted anything more delectable than her body. She's unlike any woman I've ever taken to the hotel. She doesn't belong there. It's not the place for her.

"Gabriel." Caleb's voice pulls me from my thoughts. "You're actually going to cut that little asshole a check to keep his mouth shut."

"Sit," I say hoarsely. "Sit down and shut up, Caleb."

There's no more than a moment of hesitation before he lowers himself into one of the two chairs in front of my desk. His head is shaking from side-to-side as he curses repeatedly under his breath. He's hot-headed. He's always been this way.

"Mother offered Dante Castro a position with the company," I begin before I take a large swallow from the now warm cup of coffee on my desk. "I was under the belief that it was a verbal agreement. I imagined she threw the offer out without any thought but apparently he's more astute than I've given him credit for. He drew up a simple contract on the back of a napkin while they were having lunch and he had it witnessed."

"That means nothing, Gabricl."

"It means he has leverage and this press conference he's arranged this morning to announce the lawsuit he's planning on launching will cast a negative light on us." I look past his head to the reception area where Sophia is finally settling in for the day. It's not uncommon for me to get to the office before her. It is rare for there to be this much activity before nine o'clock.

"So you're just going to give him money?" he spits the question out without looking at me. "You don't believe for a second that contract will hold up in court, do you?"

"Of course not," I pause. "It has no legal merit but that's not what I'm concerned with."

"What the hell are you concerned with then?"

I lean back in my chair, crossing my legs. "If this contract mother signed becomes public knowledge, the Berdine division is going to be

147

upended. The design team there will be pissed that she's trying to replace them and we're going to lose some of the best people we have."

"I'm inclined to push him on it." He mirrors my stance, crossing his own legs as he runs his fingers along the arm of the chair. "I say we let this play out and see where the cards fall."

"That's not happening," I continue, "Berdine is running smoother than it ever has. I see no reason to tempt fate by allowing Dante Castro to take this public. I spoke with his attorney before you got here, Caleb. I'm having the papers drawn up now and I'll sign the check this afternoon. They're cancelling his press conference as we speak."

"What makes you think you can do that?" His right hand fists. It's a faint movement but it's not lost on me. "You make these unilateral decisions for all of us. What gives you that right?"

I sigh as I feel a faint smile tugging at the corners of my lips. "I'm the CEO, Caleb. How the hell do you keep forgetting that?"

***

"She's not here, sir." Cicely motions towards the bustling sales floor. "Isla is on her lunch break."

I glance down at my watch. It's near one now. I'd spent my morning dealing not only with the loose ends of the Dante Castro debacle, but with a problem at one of the production facilities overseas. It's been a stressful day so far, and the calm from the storm I'm craving is a few minutes alone with Isla.

I need to explain what happened last night to her. I want her to understand that my body's desire to fuck her was only tamed by my need to do it any place but there. When she was nude in front of me, her slick cunt waiting to be taken, I'd stopped myself because of my own selfish yearning to take her to my bed. I want her in my bed, the bed I've never taken another woman to.

"She asked for an extra fifteen minutes, Mr. Foster." Cicely shifts on her feet. "I think she had a lunch date. A man came in to get her."

My shoulders instantly tighten. "Did she introduce you to him?"

Her gaze narrows as she studies my face. "She didn't but he's been in here before. He came in last week to buy some lingerie. Isla helped him pick it out."

Jealousy hits me full on. It's not an emotion I'm that familiar with. I can't recall the last time I felt this burning pit in my stomach. "It's a customer?"

"I think he's more than that to Isla. He hugged her when he came in the door."

"What did he look like?" I ask before I even realize I've formed the question within my mind. What the fuck does it matter what he looks like? What matters is who the hell he is to Isla.

"He's very attractive." She sighs. "He's tall, dark hair, green eyes. He was wearing a nice suit. It wasn't a suit from Berdine, sir, but you know, it was well fitted."

"Did she say where she was having lunch?" I look across the boutique to where one of the sale associates is helping two women. "What time is she scheduled to come back?"

Her eyes dart to the clock hanging on the wall behind us. "She should be walking back through the door any minute now. That is, unless she's late again. If she is, I'll handle it, sir. I can take care of it."

I toss a glance at the bank of windows that look out onto Fifth Avenue. That's when I see her. She's wearing a fitted grey dress and her hair is styled impeccably in a ponytail. As she leans forward to embrace the man she's with, I'm flooded with an instant, and unexpected, sense of relief.

CHAPTER TWENTY-FIVE

Isla

"You two know each other?" I ask with a measure of surprise in my tone.

"Garrett is a friend," Gabriel pats Mr. Ryan on the shoulder. "He's actually the cousin of my closest friend. We travel in the same circles."

I should have known that. Almost everyone I've met since I moved to Manhattan is connected to everyone else. When I contacted Garrett Ryan to help me sort through some legal issues, I had no idea that he was actually one of the most in demand probate attorneys in all of New York. He's much more competent than the attorney I'd had in Chicago. Mr. Ryan has done more for me in the past two months than any other lawyer I've hired.

"I saw Vanessa last week." Gabriel pushes his hands into the front pockets of his pants. "My mother was admitted to the hospital. Vanessa was on duty that night."

"That's right." Mr. Ryan taps his finger on his chin. "I was glad to hear Gianna was alright."

I may not be following the conversation completely but I definitely know who Vanessa is. She's Mr. Ryan's wife. He came in last week to buy something special for her birthday. She's also a nurse with a very proud husband who loves her completely.

"I should get back to work," I say quietly because I can almost feel Cicely's eyes boring a hole into the middle of my back. "I have a lot to do this afternoon."

"I'll have my assistant prepare those documents we spoke of, Isla." Mr. Ryan's hand brushes against my shoulder. "We can have them ready tomorrow and if it's more convenient, I can stop by here with her to sign them."

"No," I blurt out quickly. "I mean, I have time after work to come to your office. I can be there by four at the latest."

"I'll clear that hour for you." His eyes dart from my face to Gabriel's. "It was good to see you, Gabriel. Call me and we'll meet for a drink soon."

"Next week," Gabriel replies as he holds out his hand. "We'll find time then."

***

"I think I should be included in this meeting." Cicely crosses her arms over her chest as she stands in the doorway of the office at the back of the boutique. "I'm Isla's manager, sir. Rowan told me to take more control over the employees."

I know he's going to send her packing, but I'd rather she stay. My day, so far, has been the shits. I'd ignored his suggestion to call his driver when I was ready to leave the hotel. Instead, I'd taken the elevator down to the entrance we arrived at last night. I'd asked one of the men standing near the door to hail me a taxi. The ride back to my apartment had been bumpy and reckless. I had to hold onto the back of the seat in front of me for dear life.

Once I finally got home, I had all of fifteen minutes to get ready for work all while trying to maneuver around Cassia's questions about where I'd spent the night. I'd pulled on the last clean dress I had in my closet and tightened my hair into a ponytail. With just a bit of make-up on, I hurried back out the door and made it to work with not more than a minute to spare. I know that, for a fact, because Cicely took it upon herself to point out the time to me.

My lunch with Mr. Ryan might have been a bright spot in my day if he hadn't handed me a letter my mother had given to her attorney to pass along to me. Months ago I would have cried while reading it. Today, I just felt empty as my eyes scanned the handwritten words. On the surface, to a stranger, they'd seem heartfelt and touching. I know better though. She's flailing and the only words that I crave from my mother are the ones she'll never say to me.

"This is a private matter," he says as he takes a step towards her. "Close the door on your way out."

"Anything that concerns the boutique should include me." She actually stomps her shoe against the floor. "I'm going to stay."

"You're going to leave now." He waves her away with a brush of his hand in the air. "Close the door. Get back to the front of the store."

An audible sigh escapes her lips as she turns on her heel and walks out, slamming the door behind her.

Cicely has a bitchy attitude. Who knew? Well, actually, I did.

I look at Mr. Foster. His hair is in place. He's more composed than he was last night. He looks

153

almost exactly as he did the first time I saw him. He also looks completely different to me now that I know what it's like to kiss him and come from the sensation of his mouth on my pussy.

"I'd like to discuss what happened last night, Isla."

This day already feels much heavier than I can manage. Possibly if I hadn't read my mother's words wishing me a happy birthday, I'd feel more emotionally equipped to talk to him. The letter was filled with sentiments I wish were true but sadly, each and every one was a thinly veiled attempt to manipulate me into giving her what she wants. That has nothing to do with a relationship with me and everything to do with money.

I cross my arms over my chest. Maybe it's an attempt to shield myself from further damage. Maybe it's nothing more than my need to stay resolute in the decision I made earlier when I left the birthday card and tickets he'd given me back in his hotel room. "There's nothing to discuss, Mr. Foster. It was a mistake. I'm sorry it ever happened and it will never happen again."

CHAPTER TWENTY-SIX

Gabriel

This is the point where I typically cut my losses and walk away. I don't have these discussions with women because I've never seen a need to. Whenever I've been with a woman and the connection has charted off the course I've wanted it to stay on, I've ended things. Investing my time, and energy, into someone I know I won't see beyond a few weeks is wasteful. There is clearly no shortage of women in Manhattan. There is, however, only one Isla Lane.

"That's not true." My jaw tightens. "It was not a mistake, Isla. It was one of the most memorable evenings I've ever had."

She blinks. "You don't have to say that. I'm not going to fall apart because of this."

I don't need to hear those words to understand that.

What she doesn't understand is that I'm already falling apart because of her words.

"I apologize for leaving in a rush this morning." I move closer but she retreats towards the door in an equal step. "I was faced with a time sensitive issue. It had to be handled immediately."

"You're a busy man." She shrugs her shoulders. "I get it. You had to go."

I haven't seen her like this before. She's closed off. She's built a barrier around herself. It's there in her posture and also in the tone of her voice. She's being dismissive, bordering on curt.

"I've upset you," I offer with an outstretched hand. "Tell me what it is, Isla. Give me a chance to fix it."

Her head shakes from side-to-side. "That's not necessary. I'm sorry I came to your hotel room."

The realization hits me immediately. I say the thing I've been thinking since I saw her nude, standing by the window last night. "I'm sorry I took you to that hotel room."

Her bottom lip quivers slightly but she's quick to halt its movement with a slow pull of her top teeth across it. The action shouldn't be as sensual as it is, but how I react to her is overpowering.

"You agree that it was a mistake?" As much as she tries to contain the emotion in her voice, she can't. I hear the tremble in it, the raw reaction.

I step closer still and this time there's no movement at all on her part. "I agree that you don't belong there. I agree that I should have taken you to my penthouse."

Her hand leaps to her chest and the soft flesh that is visible above the neckline of her dress. "It wouldn't have changed anything. Things still would have gone the way they did."

"Things?" I reach forward to brush my hand over her elbow. She stiffens slightly. "What things? I don't understand."

I see the plea in her eyes the second they meet mine. Her lips move faintly as if she's trying to find the right words. I study her face. It's so vulnerable. There's something there in her stunning blue eyes that needs to be said. It's right there, buried beneath a layer of pain.

"I need to understand what I've done." I lick my bottom lip. "I can see that I've upset you. Please, Isla, explain to me what it is."

She swallows so hard that the sound is audible in the stillness of the room. "I'm just…I'm really embarrassed, sir."

"Embarrassed?" I rake my hand through my hair. I knew I'd have to backpedal to make up for leaving in such a hurry but this is something more. I embarrassed her. I made her feel insignificant somehow.

"I asked you for things," she says in a shaky breath as she closes her eyes. "I'm sorry but I wantcd those things so I asked for them. You didn't want them. I'm so humiliated."

I grab hold of her biceps and pull her into my chest, cradling her head in my hand. "Christ, Isla. No, don't think that."

She tries to pull back but I hold her tightly. "I just wanted so much."

My chest tightens with the words. She asked me to fuck her. She wanted to blow me. I turned it all down. I'd rejected her. That's the burden she's carrying. It's my rebuff.

"Isla." I wrench her back so I can look down at her face. "Beautiful, beautiful, Isla."

Her expression shifts slightly. "We don't have to talk about this. We can just forget last night. Sometimes things aren't meant to happen."

"We are meant to happen," I say the words without any hesitation. "I didn't handle myself well last night."

"I don't want you to say those things to me." She tugs herself free from my grasp and I let her. "You don't have to be kind to me. I'm not one of those girls who need that. I'm just not."

"Do you enjoy spending time with me?" I ask clearly and succinctly.

"That's not the point, Gabriel."

"It's the only point that matters, Isla. Answer the question. Do you enjoy spending time with me?"

"Yes," she spits back. "You know that I do."

I smile faintly at the concession. "Do you want to spend more time with me?"

Her mouth curves slightly. "That's a stupid question. I mean after the way I acted last night, why are you even asking me that?"

I cock a brow. "You'll learn very quickly, Isla that no question I ask is stupid. I have a reason for everything."

"What's the reason then?" The question is laced with challenge. "Tell me the reason why last night went the way it did."

I'm on her before she has a chance to respond, pushing her back, pinning her to the wall. Her breath catches as I push my body into hers.

"Look at me, Isla." I nudge her cheek with my jaw. "Look up now."

"Yes, sir." Her voice does nothing to hide her arousal as her eyes lock on mine.

I trace my lips across her cheek before I slide them over her mouth, pulling her into a deep, intense kiss. The low moan that flows from her mouth into mine sends a wave of heat right through me.

"One taste of you unraveled me, Isla," I growl into the soft skin of her neck. "I couldn't fuck you there. That's not the place you belong."

"Where do I belong?" she asks in barely more than a whisper.

"In my bed. That is the only place you belong."

CHAPTER TWENTY-SEVEN

Isla

I'm reasonably sure when I walked out of the office with my lipstick smeared all over my mouth and Gabriel's, that Cicely finally clued in to what's been going on. If she hadn't, the hard-on that he was trying to mask beneath his carefully placed right hand would have given everything away.

He'd kissed me deeply after he told me that he wanted me in his bed. That's his actual bed and not the fuck pad one. As tempted as I was to ask him about that place and exactly how many other women have ordered room service breakfast, I didn't. His past is his past and right now I'm his present. That's the only thing that matters to me.

"Are you and Mr. Foster boning?"

Boning? Is that an actual thing?

I keep hanging up the new robes that arrived today with the hope that Cicely will disappear right along with that question. Who even refers to it as boning?

"Isla, I asked you a question." She taps me on the shoulder. "I want to know about you and Mr. Foster."

I pivot on my heel to face her. I hadn't noticed that bright red headband she's wearing before now. It actually matches her dress perfectly. It does nothing to deter from the large fabric bow that is perched on her left shoulder.

"What is it? I'm really busy right now, Cicely."

"Are you and Mr. Foster doing things? You are having sex with him, aren't you?"

So far just really spectacular oral sex, thank you. Well, technically, thank you to Mr. Foster for that.

"My personal life isn't your business." I perch my hands on my waist. "What I do after work isn't your concern, Cicely."

"Did you do it in the office just now? If you did, that's my business."

"I've never had sex in this building." I wave my hand in the air. "Have you?"

"Once."

My mouth literally falls open. I feel it and I do nothing to stop it. "You've had sex in the boutique?"

"It was after hours." She points at a table covered in lace panties. "It was over there, against that table."

I rest my fingertips against my forehead. How did I get involved in this conversation and beyond that, is there a way to get that mental image out of my mind?

"Don't run to Mr. Foster and tell him that." She points her finger at me. "I'll deny it and you'll look like a fool."

My lips twist wryly. "I won't tell a soul, Cicely. Your secret is safe with me."

I mean it. I'm not even sure I could form the words to tell anyone, let alone Gabriel, about Cicely's sex life.

***

"Isla, did you ever make it to Skyn?"

I close the door of the change room with a small push of my shoulder. I feel instant relief once I hear the latch catch.

"I went there once," I admit. "I can't say it was the best experience I've ever had."

She adjusts the lace bra she's trying on. "I like the way this fits. Does it come in different colors?"

I nod slowly. "Black, violet, I think there's also a red option, but I'll need to double check that we have it in stock."

"You don't carry collars, do you?"

She's not the first customer to ask me that. She is, however, the first, and only customer, I've had who has ever talked about Skyn, that club I went to a few weeks ago in Lower Manhattan.

"I'm sorry, Tiffany, we don't."

That's the name she likes to be called. I'm not sure if it's part of her fantasy life, but it's not the name on her credit card or on her driver's license, which she had to show me to verify her identity when she opened an account with us.

If I had to wager a guess, I'd say she's at least fifteen years older than me. The first time she came in, she asked me to help her try on dozens of different bras. During the hour I spent with her she rambled on about her penchant for being tied up. It had sparked my interest immediately and when she talked about the men she'd met at Skyn, I made the mistake of asking her where the club was.

"I know a place I can get one." She gestures to her back in an effort to get me to unclasp the bra. "Do you want to come with me after work one day? It might be fun."

There's no actual protocol that states that we can't hang out with customers, especially the ones who have the same interests we do. It's not as though I can tell Cassia about what I like in bed. I tried once, two or three years ago, when I asked if she would like it if her boyfriend spanked her.

Her reaction was telling, not just the words she used but her body language. She'd laughed uncontrollably before announcing that she'd kick any guy who tried to do that to her right in his groin.

I never brought it up again after that even though it's been something I've craved since my first year of college when the boyfriend I had helped me understand the pleasure I could find in pain.

His experience was as limited as mine but together, we'd experimented and when we broke up, I felt a void that couldn't be filled with just a good fuck. I craved more and I still do.

Last night was the first time I felt so aroused under a man's touch. When Gabriel pulled my hands back and laced them together with the sash, I almost lost my balance. I practically came when he slapped my ass. It was so much, too much but I wanted even more.

"I think I'll take these two." She motions towards two bras on the bench next to us. "You'll think about my offer, won't you?"

"I will." I might. Then again, Gabriel may give me everything I need.

CHAPTER TWENTY-EIGHT

Gabriel

"Tell me about haze."

Her head pops up as her eyes skim the perimeter of the restaurant. "You want to talk about that here?"

"Is there a reason we shouldn't?" I take a small sip from the glass of wine I ordered after we were seated. Isla opted for sparkling water again. I might have joined her until I saw the dress she's wearing. It's the same one she had on at Skyn when I spotted her through the glass. Her body is on ripe and almost full display and if we weren't in the center of Axel NY right now, enjoying what I hope will be a quick dinner, I'd be fucking her raw.

"This is a public place." She rubs her hand over the back of her neck which pushes her swollen nipples against the thin fabric of her dress. What I would give to suck on one right now.

I wave the server away as he approaches to take our dinner order. "Why haze? Tell me the significance of that."

"What's your safeword?"

The subtle attempt to shift the subject from herself to me brings a smile to my lips. "We're discussing your safeword right now."

"I don't know." She reaches towards a small basket of bread in the middle of the table before she pulls her hand back. "It's just a word. It's a word I wouldn't normally say when I'm being fucked."

Hearing that word from her mouth brings my cock to immediate and full attention.

"What do you normally say when you're being fucked?"

"If you'd let me order dinner, we could eat and you might find out for yourself."

I chuckle, loudly. "Touché, Ms. Lane. Your wish is my command."

***

"I knew that it would be beautiful," she says as she takes in the view. "I imagined it would be beautiful because you're Gabriel Foster, but this is really incredible."

I reach for her hand. "I'll give you the grand tour."

She looks up and into my face. "I need to check my phone first. I'm expecting an important text."

The moment should be effectively broken by that but it's not. I heard her speaking to Garrett Ryan during dinner. The call ended with her promise to look over a document he was sending to her before night's end.

My natural instinct to understand everything in my world has kicked in but this is Isla's business and when she's ready to share, I'll be more than willing to listen, and help, if need be. I haven't asked about her dealings with Garrett, and I won't. I trust she'll offer when, and if, she feels the need.

She crosses the room towards where she'd dropped her clutch on a small table in the foyer. I watch her ass as it moves with each step of her feet. I don't know how I've controlled myself to this point. I'll need her naked and beneath me within the next ten minutes.

"I think I forgot my phone." I hear the panic in her voice. "I left it at the restaurant. It might be in the car. I need it."

I reach into my pocket to pull out my own phone. I swipe my finger across the screen before drawing up a number.

He answers on the first ring, as he always does.

"Charles, check the car. Ms. Lane has misplaced her phone. If it's not there, go back to Axel and find it."

He says something in response but I'm lost to those words and everything else as I watch Isla dump her clutch on the table, her hands frantically searching through the items.

It's all there as it was when she dropped her clutch at Skyn. Two condoms, twenty dollars, her actual driver's license this time and the handcuffs. The same shiny, new gold handcuffs rest on the table in my foyer.

I walk up behind her, reach forward and pull them into my hand just as my phone rings.

I answer the call immediately. "Thank you, Charles. I'll call down when I want you to bring the phone up."

166

She turns slowly as her delicate hand reaches for the handcuffs. She pulls on them gently.

"Take off your dress."

"Gabriel," she says in a faint whisper. "I want those back."

"The dress, Isla." I rub the cold metal of the handcuffs across her chin. "Strip for me now."

She nods slowly as her hands reach up and behind her neck to untie the string that is holding the entire dress in place. As she pulls on the knot, it drops to the floor, her beautiful full breasts now in full view.

"Your panties." I dip my chin down. "Take them off."

She kicks one heel off and then the other before she leans forward, slowly pulling down the sheer black panties she had on.

Like this, without any shoes on, she's at least a full foot shorter than I am. She's petite and curvy. Her body sensuous and ripe.

"Have you used these?" I dangle the cuffs from my index finger.

"No," she says quietly. "I bought those before...I bought them when I moved here."

I hold tight to them as I slide my jacket off, tossing it on the table, covering her belongings. "Did you bring them with you tonight for a reason?"

She doesn't answer. The only response is an increase in her breathing as she watches me loosen my tie before I yank it off and toss it onto my jacket.

"You enjoyed it when I bound your wrists the other night, didn't you?"

"Yes, sir."

My cock hardens with the words. I remove both cufflinks before I start unbuttoning my shirt. "You came so hard when I licked your sweet cunt."

Her breath hitches as her hands dive to her pussy.

"You're a slow learner, Isla." I push the shirt from my body. "Your body is mine to touch."

Her eyes roam my broad chest, stopping to rest on my firm stomach. "Is that mine to touch?"

I can't hide the smile that drifts over my lips as I unbuckle my belt. "This is all yours to touch but only when I say so. Understood?"

Her eyes stay trained to my hands as I lower my zipper. "I understand. It's all mine."

CHAPTER TWENTY-NINE

Isla

"Haze," I repeat the word back to him as I pull softly on the handcuffs around my wrists. "I remember but I won't say it. I won't need to say it."

He kisses me again, his lips lingering longer this time. After he'd pulled my legs up and around his waist, he'd carried me to his bed. This room is different than the one we shared the other night. This is decorated warmly with beautiful art and exquisite furnishings.

After he'd settled me on my back, he'd taken the handcuffs and closed one around my right wrist. I whimpered, but it wasn't out of fear. It came from a place inside that I can't control. It's excitement, laced with need and want.

He'd looped the short gold chain through one of the railings on his wrought iron headboard. He kissed my left palm and then my wrist before he closed the cuff around it.

"Are you on birth control?" His voice is deep, it's so deep.

I look to my left at the windows that overlook Central Park. I know no one can see us up here but I feel exposed, and the question isn't helping.

"I take the pill," I confess. "I have for years. Why?"

"I'd like to fuck you without a condom." He reaches into the pocket of the pants he's still wearing to pull out a foil package. "Tonight we'll use this but if you've been tested and you're clean, I'd rather not use these again."

"Haze."

His lips part into a sly smile. "What's the problem, Isla?"

"You're like crazy hot." I dip my chin towards his chiseled abs. "You must get a lot of action. I'd rather use a condom."

"I don't get as much action as you'd think." He presses his lips to my temple. "I'm tested monthly and I'm clean."

I move my head in an effort to capture his lips with mine but he pulls back. "I want you to use a condom tonight and tomorrow if you fuck me then and even a month from now if you're still fucking me."

"I have stamina, Isla." He traces his index finger over my left nipple. "Don't mistake me for a machine though. I can't fuck you for an entire month. I'll need some breaks for sustenance and sleep."

I like this side of him. It's the side that isn't confined to a tailored suit and stuck in an office in a high rise tower. "We'll negotiate, Mr. Foster."

"Perhaps," he says as he leans forward, his left hand gripping the headboard. "Tonight you'll listen to me, yes?"

"Yes."

He brushes his fingertips over my brow as he looks into my eyes. "You have the most beautiful lips I've ever seen. I've been aching to have them wrapped around my cock."

My tongue juts out at the mention of that. "Please, now?"

I watch in silence as his hands push his pants down, followed by his boxer briefs. Seeing him like this, with nothing on, in the dimmed light of this room, puts every other man I've ever been with to shame. His cock is perfect, thick and long.

His fingers glide over the entire length, stopping to cup his balls briefly before he slides himself onto the bed. He kisses me deeply before he straddles my chest.

"Haze if it's too much, Isla. Haze."

I moan the moment the plush head of his dick touches my bottom lip and as he slides it into my mouth and across my tongue, I watch as his head falls back and his eyes close.

His breath hisses out as I raise my head to take more and when his hands bolt to my hair to sync me with the rhythm of his thrusts, I groan around the thickness. The taste of him and the sound of his voice urging me to take it all makes me wet, so wet that all I want is to reach down and finger my clit so I can come.

"Fuck." He pushes the word out in a low rough moan as he pumps harder, faster and deeper until I feel and taste the flood of his release as he holds my head in place so I can take it all.

***

I look up and right at him as he walks back into the bedroom, a pair of sweatpants are the only thing he's wearing.

He'd slid down my body after he came in my mouth. I'd whimpered at the lost touch of his cock but he sensed my need to come too.

It took not more than a few minutes of his fingers touching my clit before I bucked my hips off the bed when I fell over the edge into an intense orgasm. His mouth found mine right then and as I moaned into his lips, he moved his fingers again, this time sliding two inside me, coaxing yet another climax from me.

He'd held me tightly against him then, our nude bodies pressed into one another while his lips rested on my shoulder. I'd tugged lightly on the handcuffs and without a word, he'd moved quickly to unlock them, taking the time to kiss my hands and both of my wrists.

I sat quietly as he reached for his phone to call Charles. He asked him to bring up my phone and while he tugged the sweatpants into place, I stared out at the city. Millions of people live here, each with their own unique story and yet mine is woven into Gabriel Foster's. It makes little sense but maybe that doesn't matter. Maybe this is just about enjoying these moments for what they are.

"Check your messages, Isla," he says as he hands me my phone. "The conversation you had with Garrett on the phone sounded important."

I nod as I skim my finger over the screen to open my email app. I find his message immediately and as soon as I open it, my eyes scan the text. I pop open the document, reading it each line with care.

"You look worried." His hand taps my bare knee as he sits on the edge of the bed next to me. I'd pulled a sheet around my torso when he left the room to wait for Charles, but my legs are still completely exposed.

I rest my back against the headboard balancing my phone on my thigh. "It's just some family stuff."

"Family stuff?" He leans forward, his fingers pushing the hair on my cheek back behind my ear. "Do you want to share it with me?"

I do. I want very much to do that but whatever this is between us is too nice to mess with. Dragging my family drama into this will weigh it down. It will change the dynamic. "I can handle it."

"I have no doubt that you can. Sometimes it hclps to discuss it. It lessens the burden."

"Do you have family stuff too?" I ask half-jokingly.

"My family is one fucked up mess." His brows both jump up. "You must know that. It's all over the tabloids."

"All I know is your dad is marrying some crazy tall model."

"Crazy is the operative word, Isla." He rolls his eyes. "Bat shit crazy."

I laugh aloud. "Do people know you're this funny?"

"What people?" He edges closer to me. "You're not going to tell these people that I'm not only funny but scared shitless of heights, are you?"

"I knew it." I slap my hand against his bare shoulder. "I knew you were scared of heights."

His eyes float to the red mark on his skin. "You didn't just slap me, did you? Tell me that didn't happen."

I hear the slight change in his tone the moment I see the intensity in his glare. "I'm sorry?"

"You're sorry?" he parrots back. "It's supposed to be a statement, not a question."

"Is it?"

A ghost of a grin floats over his lips as he rips the sheet away from me, tosses my phone on the bed and flips me onto my stomach.

His lips brush over my ass cheek mere seconds before I feel the harsh sting of his hand as he slaps me in the same spot. I cry out and again when his hand connects with my flesh, harder this time.

I push my ass into the air, wanting more, craving not only the pain but the sound that escapes his lips when he hears my response. It's deep, low and wrapped around a litany of curse words.

"Please," I say into the sheets. "Again, please."

The only response I hear is the unmistakable sound of a condom package being ripped open and a moan as his hand brushes my pussy.

He yanks me back with both hands on my hips before he edges the wide crest of his cock along my folds.

"Your body is ready for me. You're wet, so wet."

I push my face against the sheet as I feel him slide inside.

174

"God, Isla." He pushes himself into me, inch by delicious inch, stretching me. "You're too tight. It's too much."

I nudge my ass back, wanting more. Sucking in a deep breath I feel him slide all the way in, the painful bite is so intense I can barely move.

Using his hands on my hips, he controls our rhythm. It's slow at first, restrained by my body's own need to adjust to his size and his command of my pleasure.

I start to move, pushing back to meet each of his thrusts. He speeds the plunges, his right foot darting to the bed to give him more depth.

I cry out from the intensity of it and as he slams himself into mc over and over again, I faintly hear my own voice calling his name as I come around his cock before he pulls my hair into his fist and rides me towards his own shaking orgasm.

CHAPTER THIRTY

Gabriel

There was a moment when the confession was mine to make. It happened when I first saw the handcuffs on the table as she rooted through her belongings trying to find her phone. It's been the one thing that has gnawed at me since I kissed her that first night in my car.

I saw her at Skyn. I watched her through the glass and I should tell her that.

Those are the words my conscience believes are my truth.

The wise, and experienced, crevices of my mind are telling me to leave it the fuck alone. She's here, in my bed, sleeping as her nude body is pressed against mine. I've tasted her, I've fucked her and I have no intention of stopping.

Drudging up a moment in the past will only embarrass her and push her back into that corner of humiliation she felt at the hotel when I ignored her pleas for more.

I have no reason to go back to that club and I'll make damn sure she doesn't either. I'll give her everything she needs and wants. Everything.

She stirs slightly, her soft breasts pressing against my chest.

I could take her again right now. If she'd given me the go ahead, I'd roll her onto her back to sink my cock into her cunt so I can feel the slickness and smoothness around me. It's something I'd only done once or twice when I was a teenager with women whose names I can't recall. The sensation was nice, pleasant but I know with Isla it would be more.

It's not what she wants. She's cautious, wary, and careful with herself.

I won't push. I want to push for more than she's ready or willing to give but she's setting the pace of this. It moves as she wishes. I don't need to tell her that, she senses it. I sense it's exactly what she needs.

"Do you have any ice cream?"

Her body trembles as it absorbs the vibrations from my chest as I chuckle deeply. "Are you talking in your sleep or do you want ice cream?"

"You're so ripped I bet you never eat ice cream."

I roll over her, pinning her hands against the sheet above her head. Her hair is a mess, her lips still swollen from when I'd fucked her mouth hours ago.

"I have chocolate and strawberry." I inch her thighs apart with my knee. "If you want another flavor, I'll send Charles to get it."

"You'd send him to get me ice cream?"

"I'll go myself if you prefer." I look down at her body. It's beautiful.

She circles her hips off the bed. "I don't want you to go."

"I'll stay here forever if that's what you want."

Her eyes soften as she stares into mine. It's almost painful the way she looks at me. There's a pureness there, an innocence that is in sharp contrast to the person she presents to the world. Here, with me, there's no filter in her smile or her gaze.

"I'll get you any flavor of ice cream you want after I make love to you."

Her eyes inch down my face to my chest and beyond. "Do you have another condom? I brought some. They're on the table by the door."

I nod faintly when I inch closer, leaning forward to run my tongue over her bottom lip.

"Please, get the condom." She pulls her hands free to push at my chest. "I can't. I won't without it."

I hike her thighs over mine and scoop my hand behind her back as I lean to the left to grab the condom package I'd placed on the nightstand earlier. I rest her back down as I rip it open to sheath myself, my eyes glued to her face the entire time.

"I'm sorry," she says softly. "It's just that…"

"No." I silence her with a finger to her lips. "You will never apologize for protecting yourself."

She nods faintly.

Her thighs are still splayed across mine as I inch forward rubbing the head of my dick over her clit. "You come first. I will never push for more than you can give. Do you understand that?"

"Yes," she says the words breathlessly as I slide into her. "I understand."

I don't say another word as I lower my mouth to hers and fuck her with a tenderness that I've never felt before.

***

"You're full of secrets, aren't you?"

Her voice startles me. I'm sitting in my home office. Dawn hasn't broken yet and when she'd had her fill of ice cream and me, she'd finally fallen into a deep sleep. I'd kissed her softly before I pulled myself from the bed to make a call to our European head office in Rome. I'd spoken as quietly as I could so as not to wake her.

"You're not an undercover reporter doing a story on my family, are you?" I smooth my hands over the sweatpants I'm wearing again. "Come, sit here."

She walks over quickly, her body covered by the dress shirt I wore to dinner. I prefer it on her, even though her hands have disappeared beneath the fabric of the arms.

I adjust her into the perfect spot before I circle my hands around her waist. "What new secret have you uncovered, Ms. Lane?"

"Secrets," she corrects me with a soft kiss to the mouth. "As in more than one."

I claim her mouth again, this time tracing my tongue over her bottom lip. "Tell me about these secrets."

"The first is that you're reading that new detective novel that everyone is talking about on social media." She trails her index finger over my chin.

"You saw it on the nightstand. That's hardly a secret."

"That's not the actual secret." She slides her hand to the back of my neck so she can pull me into a long, lingering kiss. "The secret is that you read the last page before you'd even finished the third chapter because you were so anxious to know the ending."

"Parli Italiano?"

"Yes," she whispers into my cheek. "I speak Italian."

"How much of that conversation did you hear?" I try to sound stern but it's futile. "More importantly, where did you learn to speak Italian?"

"I heard the last few minutes of it." She nuzzles her face into the crux of my neck. "I wasn't eavesdropping. You weren't in bed so I wanted to find you."

"I'm glad you did."

"My grandmother spoke Italian." She runs her fingers over my chest. "She loved an Italian man desperately when she was my age."

"So your grandfather is Italian?" I ask, pulling her even closer to me.

"No, the Italian man loved an Italian woman. My grandmother married a man from Ireland."

I laugh loudly. "Did the Irish man make her happy?"

"He was Irish." She tilts her head up to look into my eyes. "What do you think?"

"I think she loved him enough to marry him so he made her very happy."

"He did." She nods faintly as she cups my cheek. "Until the day he died."

CHAPTER THIRTY-ONE

Isla

"That's only one secret, Isla." He brushes his cheek against my forehead as I rest my head on his chest. "What's the other secret?"

This one is harder. It's not playful and fun. It's also not my business but I don't do well with curiosity. It eats at me. It's only a question. The worst that can happen is that he'll tell me it's none of my business.

"It's about your fuck pad."

"Fuck. Pad," he says the words separately, decisively. "What is that?"

I sigh heavily in jest as I look into his eyes. "It's the place you take all the ladies to when you want to nail them."

His brows cock in unison. "Nail them? No. Don't. My brother talks like that."

I smile at the expression on his face. "We'll start over. I have a question about the hotel room that you use to fuck women."

"Why are we talking about that?" He shifts beneath me. "It's a hotel that is owned by my family. I use the room occasionally to entertain."

"Call it what you will." I tap his shoulder. "I don't care about that. I was wondering about the bedroom."

"What about it?" I hear the uneasiness in his tone.

181

"There's a chest of drawers there. It's locked."

He scrubs the back of his neck with his palm. "Yes, I keep that locked."

"What's in it?"

He leans back, slightly breathless. That reaction should be all the answer I need but it's not. "I'd rather not discuss this, Isla. At least not right now."

His legs move beneath me. I stand up sensing that he needs me to. "That's fine. I was just curious."

He rises to his feet too. "We need to preface that conversation with one about your experiences."

"My experiences?" My hands leap to my chest. "I'm not sure I'm following. What experiences?"

"You enjoy being bound," he says quietly. "Restrained."

I nod, shifting nervously on my feet.

He rakes both hands through his hair. "You responded when I spanked you. Pain gets you off?"

"It depends who is administering it," I confess. "I liked when you did it."

"What else do you enjoy?" He drops his hands to sides. "Tell me what else you've done that you've liked."

This isn't the discussion I anticipated when I walked into his office. I honestly thought he'd tell me that he keeps dildos in those drawers to use on the women he brings there. The worst thing I imagined was that he'd confess to me that he collects the used panties he's ripped off all the women he's fucked there. I never imagined this would be turned around on me.

"I was in a sex swing once." I dart my index finger into the air. "That was hot."

His hands jump to his lips. "I'll keep that in mind. What else?"

"I once sucked a man off on a bus," I begin. "It was late and dark but…"

"No." His chest heaves. "I don't mean that." "You asked." My hands dart to my hips. "I'm just telling you what I've done."

Before I can react his hands are on my biceps, gripping, tugging. "Have you ever been flogged, Isla? Has a man ever whipped you? Have you ever come from having hot wax dripped onto your skin?"

I shake my head slowly, ever so slowly from side-to-side.

"Nipple clamps? You've used though, yes?" "No, sir."

"That's what is in those drawers, Isla. Those are the things I keep there, they are what I enjoy."

I lace my fingers together in front of me. "I've never done that, any of that."

He closes his eyes. "I didn't want this conversation to happen now. I would never have chosen to share these things this way, this early. "

I should say that I want to try, or at the very least, that I want to know more, but I can't. Not yet. Not when I'm uncertain that I have the internal strength to do any of it.

"Can I go home now?" I ask quietly. "I think I should go home."

"No." His voice is edged with a plea, just as his expression is. "Let's go back to bed. Let me hold you until morning. Please, Isla."

I should have stayed there, wrapped in the sheets that still held the scent of our lovemaking. If I had done that, this wouldn't be stuck in the air between us now.

"I'll stay until morning." I reach for his hand. "I'll stay."

***

"I need you to understand something." He's on his knees next to the bed as I open my eyes after falling back asleep. "I have to explain something to you before I take you home."

I roll onto my side so I'm facing him directly. I tuck my hands next to my face. "What is it, Gabriel?"

"You have the most melodic voice I've ever heard." He brushes my hair from my forehead. "You're a good singer, aren't you?"

I smile. "I can't hold a tune. I'm a fantastic violinist though."

"The best I've ever heard." He licks his bottom lip. "I've never met anyone quite like you before."

"That's because there's only one me."

He laughs. "You have no idea how true that statement is."

"I've never met anyone like you before either." I swallow past the lump in my throat. "Last night was amazing. I've never had a night like that."

"I need to say something about what happened in my office." His voice is still sleepy. "The things I spoke of don't define my desires."

"You like them though."

"I find them arousing."

I wipe the back of my hand over my eyes, trying desperately to chase the sleep away. "The first time my boyfriend tied me to the bed, I was scared."

His expression softens as he traces his index finger over my chin. "Did you tell him that?"

I exhale harshly. "I did and he assured me. He got on the bed next to me. He held me close. He told me he'd take care of me and we choose a safeword together."

"Haze?"

"No. It was something else. I don't remember anymore what it was."

He presses a kiss to my forehead. "Did you use your safeword during that encounter?"

"I didn't have to." I look up and into his eyes. "He was gentle. It was a fantastic experience."

"Did he spank you?"

"Not that time, later, other times."

He hesitates for a moment. "Tell me why you like the spanking. How does it feel?"

I duck my head down for a moment to shield the blush I feel racing over my cheeks. I've spoken about intimacy to men before, but not like this, not with this level of vulnerability. No one has ever tried to understand me this way.

"It feels freeing; almost like I'm letting go." I rub my thighs together. "There's also the physical part of it. My pussy trembles when I'm spanked. Everything feels so much more sensitive."

"It can be that way with a flogger, or a crop too. Those sensations, you can feel them more intensely under the skilled hand of a man who knows how to push you to the edge."

"Do you want to do those things to me, Gabriel?"

In one fluid movement he's on the bed, his hands braced on either side of me, his face hovering close to mine. "I want to give you the most intense pleasure you've ever experienced. Whether I use my hand, my mouth, my cock, or anything else hardly matters. I just want you to feel as much as you can under my touch."

I want that too. I want to tell him that but I can't. It's all too much.

"I told you I'd never push for more than you can give, Isla. I meant that."

"I know that you did."

"Will you promise me one thing?"

If he'd look at me the way he is now for every day of the rest of my life, I'd promise him anything. "What is it?"

"Promise me that you'll let me take you to the symphony tomorrow night as planned." His lips graze my cheek. "Let me see you experience that."

"There's no one else in the world I'd rather go with than you."

CHAPTER THIRTY-TWO

Gabriel

"Why are you smiling? You never fucking smile." Caleb gestures over the small table in the crowded café at me. "You're nailing someone, aren't you?"

This time the vile word actually brings an even wider smile to my lips. "Don't be crude, Caleb. I'm seeing someone."

"Seeing, nailing, screwing, call it whatever the fuck you want."

"Seeing. I'm dating a remarkable woman." I take another bite of the sandwich I'd ordered before he arrived. I'd suggested lunch in the office, this hole in the wall was his idea.

He looks past me to the expansive menu scrawled across a chalkboard hanging over the open kitchen. "I'm starving. Give me half of your sandwich."

"Order your own," I say mid chew. "You should get in line now if you're going to make it back to the office before our meeting."

"We need to discuss dad." He drops his gaze from the menu to my face. "He's jumping into this marriage thing without a life boat."

"A life boat?" I swallow a mouthful of water. "It's another euphemism for sex, isn't it? If it is, I don't want to talk about it."

He pulls a half-eaten candy bar from the inner pocket of his suit jacket. He takes a large bite. "There's no prenup. He's marrying her without anything in place."

Even my father wouldn't be foolish enough to do that. "You're mistaken. Roman is smarter than that."

"Roman is pussy whipped right now."

I drop my sandwich on the paper plate in front of me. "I told you never to talk about that. I don't want to know who he's sleeping with."

He reaches across the table to pull my sandwich into his hand. He folds open the bread, pulling out a soggy tomato. "He's marrying her, Gabriel. Don't tell me you think she's hopping on that train for his mad skills in the sack. He's giving it to her alright but it's all about the money."

"How do you know there's no prenup?" I finish the last mouthful of water from the plastic bottle I'd ordered with the sandwich. "Who told you that?"

"Dear old dad did." He chews heartily. "He called me up this morning to share that tidbit of information with me."

"You told him he's lost his mind right?"

"I told him she was screwing his brains out for what's in his wallet, or more accurately, what's in our collective wallets since dad still owns a share in the company."

"Is he getting a lawyer?" I scroll my fingers over the screen of my smartphone. "I can call one right now to handle this."

188

"He's dead set against it. According to pops, she's the love of his life."

I push my hands against the edge of the table and stand. "Bring that with you. We're going back to the office. It's time we had a discussion with Caterina Omari."

"You're going to cut her a check too, aren't you?" He drops the remainder of the sandwich back on the paper plate. "That's how you're going to make her disappear."

"You can't put a price on love, Caleb." I button my suit jacket. "If she takes the bait, we've saved Roman from that shark. He'll thank us…eventually."

***

"I need you to get Caterina Omari on the phone." I gaze down at Sophia, who is just finishing her own lunch which, judging from the crumbs and crust, was a slice of pizza. "Where did you get that pizza?"

"Why?" She tosses the paper cup filled with soda that was just in her hand in the trashcan. "I'm allowed to eat lunch at my desk, sir, aren't I?"

"It smells delicious." I tilt my head to the left. "You'll order that for us both tomorrow."

A small smile pulls at the corners of her mouth. "I can do that, sir."

"Who died?" Caleb walks back out of my office to stand in the open doorway. He'd walked right past Sophia without a second glance when we stepped off the elevator. Much of that had to do with the fact that he was absorbed in a phone conversation with his wife.

"Someone died?" Sophia's hand jumps to her chest. "Shall I send flowers, sir?"

Caleb knocks on the doorframe. "It looks like someone already did. You're the one who accepts deliveries for Gabe, aren't you?"

"Gabriel." I toss him a look. "What are you talking about?"

"There's a bouquet of dead flowers on your desk. Either someone died or you pissed someone off. Either way, I need to run. Rowan is on her way to my office."

He pats me on the back as he brushes past me on his way back to the elevator.

"There was a delivery, sir." Sophia rises to her feet. "I'm sorry but I didn't realize the flowers were dead. I can remove them right now."

"No." I wave her back down with my hand as I catch sight of the bouquet of stunning black tulips in a large vase on my desk. "Hold my calls. I'll buzz when I wish to speak with Caterina."

"Certainly, sir."

CHAPTER THIRTY-THREE

Isla

"Your mother's attorney called this morning."
Mr. Ryan nods to his assistant as he places a cup of
coffee in front of him. "Are you sure you don't want
something to drink, Isla?"

I don't. I had two cups of coffee this morning
with Cassia before we both left for work which is two
cups too many for me. I have exactly an hour for this
meeting before I have to back from lunch. I want this
to be over quickly. "I'm fine, Mr. Ryan."

"Garrett." He smiles softly. "You need to start
calling me Garrett."

My gaze drops to the stack of papers he'd
placed in front of me when I sat down. "What did her
attorney say?"

"I'm obligated to tell you this by law." He
leans back in his chair, crossing his legs. "If I wasn't
required to do that, I wouldn't bring it up."

I scratch my cheek. "It's another settlement
offer, isn't it?"

"It is." He reaches forward to grab the coffee
mug. "It's not worth talking about. I see no reason to
entertain any offer from them."

I haven't until now either. Up to this point, the
money that I've been receiving from the account that
my grandmother set up in my name has been limited
to a few hundred dollars a month. It was meant to
cover my expenses while I attended Juilliard. She had

191

little doubt in her mind that I'd study there and the small offering from her estate was for covering my everyday expenses. A lot has changed now that I'm twenty-one. I'm now entitled to receive everything she willed to me.

"What if I settled with her?" I smooth my hands over the skirt of my dress. "If I did that, she'd drop her lawsuit, right?"

"Your mother's lawsuit has no merit, Isla." He sits upright in his chair. "Your grandmother's will was very clear. Your half-sisters each receive a small lump sum when they reach twenty-one. You inherit all of her properties, investments, and the remainder of her estate."

I don't need to hear that. I've heard it over and over from countless attorneys. The numbers may change slightly as the stocks rise and fall but the bulk of it is several homes in different corners of the world and more money than anyone can spend in their lifetime.

My grandmother and grandfather worked hard their entire lives and when combined with the wealth she inherited when her own father died, it's accumulated to what could be a life of leisure for me. That's not my intention though. My intention is to carry on my grandmother's legacy, including her dream of being a principal violinist with the New York Philharmonic.

"I want this to be over." I tap the top of the papers. "You've already told me that this may drag on for years and years."

"It's a possibility," he admits. "Eventually the case will be heard before a judge. I have no doubt that you'll be awarded everything your grandmother left you."

"My grandmother's heart was so soft." I swallow to curb the emotions I'm feeling. "She loved my mother, but she was disappointed in her."

"Your mother made some unforgiveable decisions." He coughs into his hand. "You know how I feel about the funds that were transferred from your trust account to her."

He's talking about the money I made when I was a child. The truth of what she'd done with that became evidence in the lawsuit that my mother launched more than two years ago in anticipation of my twenty-first birthday and the day I'd inherit everything.

Mr. Ryan has urged me time, and time again, to countersue my mother for that money. I can't do it. It's just money. It will never replace what I lost. I'll never again have a relationship with my mother that is based on trust and unconditional love.

"You can make a counter offer, can't you?" I inch forward in my chair. "You can offer less than she's asking for."

"Isla." He folds his hands together on his desk. "I discourage this, strongly. It wouldn't be a wise move on your part."

"It would end all of this." I wave my hand over the stack of papers in front of me. "It would stop this forever, right?"

"Your mother would have to sign off on the agreement, yes. It would be clear and final."

"What about my sisters?" Hearing myself refer to them that way is hard. My mother has

193

poisoned their memories to the point that neither will even acknowledge I exist. "It wouldn't impact their inheritances, would it?"

"No, not at all." He looks at me. "It would have no bearing on them at all."

"Please present them with a counter offer." I hold up my hand to halt him. "I've considered everything you've told me, but this is my life. I want to get on with it. I want this to be over. Please help me make that happen."

CHAPTER THIRTY-FOUR

Gabriel

"You sent your driver to get me." She brushes past me as she walks into my office. "Cicely had a million questions about that."

"I'm sure she did." I close the doors, noting Sophia's empty chair. I'd sent her away with a list of mundane errands I've been putting off. I don't want any interruptions.

"You look beautiful, Isla."

Her eyes drop to the blue wrap dress she's wearing. "Thank you, sir. Are you going to fire me?"

I try to contain the smile I feel on my lips. "Fire you? Have you done something that warrants that?"

She rubs her index finger under her nose, just above her top lip. "Is there a rule about opening your dress and showing a customer your lingerie?"

My hand leaps to my tie. The air in the room suddenly feels thick and stifling. "When did that happen?"

"This morning," she says sheepishly.

"You opened this dress and showed someone your body?"

"Yes." She smiles, leaning against the corner of my desk. "I showed my bra and panties to a customer."

"A woman?" I ask half-jokingly, trying to will away my erection. I didn't call her here for this but now that she's confessing, I can't concentrate on anything but what's under her dress.

Her hands drop to the belt of the dress. "I know there's a rule about not taking a man in the change rooms. There's not a rule about displaying the lingerie you're wearing in the middle of the boutique, is there?"

My own hand drops to the front of my pants. I adjust my belt. "Did you show a man your lingerie, Isla? Did you let a man see your beautiful body?"

"What would happen to me if I did?" she asks quietly. "You'd punish me, wouldn't you?"

Why the fuck can't I tell if she's toying with me or not?

"Open your dress." I lower my voice. "Show me what you showed him."

Her delicate fingers make quick work of the sash, undoing the double knot and bow. She holds the dress closed in front of her, the only hint of what's beneath is a sliver of blue lace visible in the middle of her chest.

"Open the dress," I repeat. "Take it off."

"You got my flowers." She pivots on her heel so she's facing my desk. "Do you like them?"

I'm behind her before she can react, my hands inside the front of the dress, skimming across her stomach. "They're black tulips, Isla. You sent me black tulips."

She pushes her body back into mine, grinding her ass against me. "Do you know why I choose those?"

196

I glide my hand down her smooth stomach to the top of her panties. "They symbolize power and strength."

She nods, her hands moving to cover mine. "You're those things to me. That's how I see you."

"The card," I whisper the words into her ear as I slide my hand over her thigh. "The card took my breath away."

She picks it up, cradling it in her fingers. "I want to be under your touch. Isla."

"Under my touch," I repeat the words back to her, my fingers over the panties now, feeling the heat of her arousal through the lace.

She moans, softly. "I could come from that touch."

"Turn around."

I feel the hesitation in her entire body as she pulls away from my hands and twists around so she's facing me. I stare down at her face. Her makeup is exactly as it was the first day I saw her at the boutique. It's dark, the contours make her look untamed and edgy.

I cup her ass with one hand, the other moves quickly to her back as I pick her up and turn her, moving until she's flat on her back on the leather sofa, her dress open to reveal a light blue bra and panties.

I brace one hand on the back of the sofa, the other next to her shoulder. "I will punish you if you opened this dress to show another man this. Tell me that didn't happen, Isla."

Her lips move faintly before her tongue darts out to moisten them. "You can see my nipples and my pussy, can't you? The lace is very thin."

My eyes travel slowly over the length of her. Every intimate part of her is visible through the thin, blue lace. There is absolutely nothing left to the imagination. "Tell me who you showed this to and I'll kill him with my bare hands."

She laughs loudly, her hand flying to her mouth to shelter the sound. "You wouldn't kill a man for looking at my body. You're not that intense, Gabriel."

I reach down to cup her chin in my hand. "Keep your clothes on at work, Isla. This is only for me. Understood?"

Her eyes fall to my body. "That's all for me, right? Only me? You're not going to your fuck pad this week, are you?"

I fall to one knee as I slowly pull her panties down. "There is one woman and one woman only that I intend to spend my time with."

Her ass moves as I lower my mouth to her stomach, tracing a path across the soft flesh with my tongue. A soft moan falls from her lips as I graze my mouth over her cunt.

"You are all that I want, Isla." I breathe in her scent. "This is all that I want."

Her hands grip my hair as I pull open her legs, wrap my lips around her swollen clit and lick and suck her until she comes under my touch.

CHAPTER THIRTY-FIVE

Isla

"That's a beautiful dress, Isla." Cassia stands in the doorway of my room, wearing one of Nigel's t-shirts and his sweatpants. "Do you have a date?"

"I do," I try to quiet the anxiety in my voice. "I'm going to the symphony."

"Your date knows you really well." She laughs. "Nigel knows better than to take me there."

I've never absorbed her disinterest in classical music as anything other than what it actually is. Cassia likes dress pants and blouses. I like dresses and skirts. She likes computers and offices. I like my violin and a place to play it. We're different, very different, but our friendship is what binds us together.

"Can we talk before you go?" She shifts her sock covered feet on the hardwood floors. "It's kind of important."

"Sit." I gesture towards my bed. "Is something wrong? Your folks are okay, right?"

I only ask because her father had a scare with his heart three months ago. He was walking the family dog one night and doubled over in pain. Cassia had been on the first flight back to Chicago and when she finally called to tell me that it had been a minor heart attack that required a change in diet and a simple medical procedure, I'd been relieved.

I don't know my own father. My mother always told me that he was a bastard one night stand so I've loved Cassia's vicariously through her. He sends me text messages sometimes just to see how I am. I treasure those, just as I cherish her entire family.

"They're good. They both send their love for your birthday." She rubs her hand over her eyes. "They'll take you out for dinner the next time they're in New York."

That would be the first time. They've never come here. I doubt they ever will. They love Chicago. It's where they belong.

"What's wrong?" I lower myself to the corner of the bed. "Is it Nigel?"

She sets her hands on her thighs. "He asked me to marry him."

My eyes dart down to her empty left hand. There's no ring. I ask even though the answer is obvious. "What did you say?"

"I love him," she confesses softly. "Maybe I didn't realize how much until he asked me to be his wife."

"You're going to marry him?" I hear the shock in my own voice, there's no possible way she won't pick up on it.

She smiles, revealing her perfect teeth. "Not yet. One day I think I will."

"He's okay with that?"

Her hands reach to grab one of mine. "I'm going to move in with him, Isla. We're going to get a place together, that's just for us."

Relief wouldn't have been the first emotion I expected, but it's what's there. The surprise is buried beneath it.

"I hate to do this to you." She gestures towards the hallway. "I know how expensive this place is and I know how hard it will be to find a new roommate."

I can afford it. I can turn her bedroom into a music room. The acoustics aren't great but it's a place I can practice without fear of disturbing anyone. I can cook. I can read. I can be me, just me.

I move so I can pull her into a hug. "I'm so happy for you, Cassia. Don't worry about me. I have a feeling I'm going to be just fine."

***

"Thank you for bringing your violin tonight," Gabriel says as he carries it in his left hand. His right is holding one of mine. "I was hoping that you'd give me a private concert."

I look up and into his face. He'd been just as entranced with the symphony's performance as I had been. He'd held my hand throughout and once the room had cleared, he'd kissed me there in the orchestra seats, telling me that he loved how I leaned forward in my seat the entire night. My eyes were half closed as I listened to the music.

"I'd love to play for you." I step into the elevator before he does. "Do you have a special request?"

"You'll play your favorite piece for me."

I knew he would say that before the words left his lips. He's demanding and intimidating in business, but when he's with me, he wants to see the world through my eyes. I sense that. I feel it more and more each time we're together.

"I will. Do you want me to do that when we get up to your place?" I watch the lights on the panel as the car travels towards the top floor.

"I want to punish you for what you did in my office yesterday." There's a dark bite in his tone.

"I came twice. How does that deserve a punishment, sir?"

His hand jumps to his lips. I know he's trying to shield a smile. "I'm talking about what happened prior to that. You have yet to tell me if you really showed your body to a customer."

"There are security cameras in the boutique." I grab the rail as the elevator jars to a stop. "Why don't you check for yourself?"

CHAPTER THIRTY-SIX

Gabriel

"You're a tease, Isla." I carefully place the violin case on the table near the door.

"A cock tease." She turns towards me as she pulls on the hem of the simple black dress she's wearing. "Or just a tease."

"Both," I say under my breath as I slide my suit jacket off. "I'm having a scotch. What can I get you?"

"Water."

I walk into the kitchen and pour myself a scotch, neat, and then drop a few ice cubes in a tumbler before opening a bottle of sparkling water to empty half into the glass. I take them back to where she's now seated on the sofa.

She takes the tumbler, drinking a quarter of the liquid before she pulls a piece of ice between her teeth and pops it into her mouth. She's by far the most sensual woman I've ever been with. What makes it even more erotic is that she isn't aware of her charm.

"Tell me why you don't drink." I sip the scotch. "I commend it, but you once mentioned that you were avoiding alcohol because it makes you foggy. I believe that's the word you used."

The ice cube pops out momentarily before she sucks it back onto her tongue.

Jesus. How is this making me hard?

"I went to a club one night." She bites the ice cube. "I used a fake ID to get in."

"There's obviously more to this story." I lean back, crossing my legs.

She picks up the glass and drinks more of the water. "I was partying hard, like way too hard. I almost did some stuff with a dentist."

"A dentist?" I ask, leveling my tone. She means that asshole that had his hands all over her at Skyn. Fuck that bastard for touching her.

"Supposedly." She arches a brow. "It's the kind of club where you don't ask a lot of questions."

"No questions." I sip more scotch.

She reaches back to scratch her neck; the motion graceful and compelling. Her entire torso stretches, pushing her breasts forward. "You have to ask some questions I guess. I don't know a lot about the place but there's a rumor that people fuck in the back rooms."

"So you went there to fuck?" I stiffen in my seat.

My window of opportunity to tell her that I was behind the mirrored glass watching her is closing. The need I have to hear her tell the story is too much. She'll never know I was there. The contracts signed upon entry to the backrooms guarantee that even if we run into someone who recognizes me from Skyn, my secret is safe with them.

"A customer told me about the club." She plays with a thread that has come loose on the hem of her dress. "She told me people go there who like the things I do."

"People who enjoy being fucked in sex swings?"

"You're going to get one of those, aren't you?" Her face brightens. "God, your cock and a swing. I'd never leave this place."

"I'll have one here within the hour if that's the case."

She smiles wildly before her eyes fall back to her lap. "I went there because the customer from the boutique told me that her husband ties her up sometimes and they met there."

Christ. She went to Skyn to find a man to bind her. She walked right into the middle of a lion's den.

"Did you find what you were looking for there?" I ask because selfishly I want to hear it. I want her to say the words. I want her to say that she found it in the boutique, or in my office, or in my fucking bed.

She swallows quickly before she looks at me. "I wish that night had never happened. I humiliated myself. I was drunk, and if one of the women who work there hadn't come to my rescue, I would have done things I regretted, probably for the rest of my life. She saved me."

I finish the rest of my drink quickly as I stare at her face wishing I could tell her that we actually saved each other that night.

***

"Do you have a crop here?" she whispers the question into the stillness of the room as she sits patiently on the edge of the bed completely nude, waiting for me to undress. "Do you keep all that at the hotel or is some of it here?"

I crouch down in front of her, pushing her legs apart. "Tell me what you think of me."

"What?" Her hands leap to my cheeks, cradling them. "What does that mean?"

"When I look at you," I begin before I cup my hand over one of hers, pressing her soft skin into my face. "I see this incredibly sensual woman who wants to explore and experience things. I see someone who is very comfortable with her body and isn't afraid to experiment."

"I like sex," she admits. "I've always liked it since I first had it."

"When you look at me what do you see?" I sweep my hand over her forehead, pushing her hair aside. "Tell me."

Her blue eyes study my face, her hands sliding over the contours of my jaw, my nose and my brows. "I see someone who is patient and kind."
"Don't tell those people you always speak of about that," I tease. "That's our secret."

She leans forward to brush her soft lips against mine. "I won't tell a soul."

"What else do you see?"

She exhales audibly, her tiny frame tremoring from the movement. "If I asked you something, would you tell me the answer, honestly?"

"Without hesitation."

"Am I special?" Her soft voice cracks with the words. "Will you remember me?"

The sharp pain in my chest almost doubles me over. I rise from my feet, push her back onto the bed, and kiss her deeply, slowly.

"You're the most amazing person I've ever known," I murmur into her lips as I pull back from the kiss. "I want to know you forever. I'll never forget you."

CHAPTER THIRTY-SEVEN

Isla

"I think ten of me could fit in your bathtub." I blow on the fragrant bubbles around me. "This is really expensive bubble bath, isn't it? It's lavender. Do you bathe in this?"

He laughs loudly as he swings his large legs over the edge of the tub before lowering himself into the water. "I bought this for you earlier today, Isla. I shower. I don't generally bathe."

"Did you get more ice cream?" I move towards him, clearing a path through the bubbles so I can float into his arms.

"Two pints." He pulls me closer as I wrap my thighs around his waist. "I'll feed it to you after our bath."

I look around the large room. He'd lit candles while I was still in the bed and he'd turned on music that is quietly filling the space. It's Bach, a favorite of his I think.

"Have you always lived alone?" I rub the pad of my thumb over his jaw, brushing away a bubble.

"Since I moved away for college." He squeezes my ass. "I never did the roommate thing. You don't talk about your roommate often."

"She's not going to be my roommate after next Friday." I lean back into his hand, wanting him to touch my pussy the same way he did in the bed earlier before he fucked me.

208

He acquiesces, his long fingers stroking my clit beneath the surface of the water. "What happens after next Friday?"

I close my eyes as I move on his hand. "She's moving out."

He reaches up to cup my breast with his free hand, pulling and twisting my nipple. "Are you going to get a new roommate?"

"That spot," I groan. "Why does that feel so good?"

"Your cunt is so sensitive, Isla." He kisses me softly. "It's so plush, so greedy and wet."

I can't focus on anything but my desire to come again. I move forward when the thickness of his hard cock rubs against my ass. "I love when you fuck me."

"Let yourself go." His breath is a whisper against my neck. "Let yourself feel."

I grab hold of his biceps, pushing my fingernails into his rock hard muscles as I grind my pussy into his hand and fall over the edge crying out his name.

***

"Are you going to get a new roommate, Isla?" He places the empty ice cream container and two metal spoons on the nightstand. "I can help you find someone suitable."

"You mean someone without a cock?"

He chuckles. "I'd prefer if you didn't live with a man, but it's your choice, of course."

I know that he means that. I can't imagine he'd ever tell me what to do or what decisions to make. I do want his guidance though. He's educated in areas that I have little experience in.

"Can we talk about something?" I close my eyes briefly to chase away my doubts. "It's something personal."

He lowers himself back to the bed so he's facing me directly. He pulls a corner of the sheet over his lap, shielding his body. I'm grateful. Telling him about my life while staring at his cock, would be a welcome, but awkward, distraction.

"We can talk about anything you'd like. Tell me what it is."

His phone rings. The sound startles me enough that I pull the sheet tighter around me. Maybe it's a sign. Maybe I'm not supposed to feel so comfortable with him that I'm sharing my innermost secrets.

He doesn't move. He doesn't even flinch as it continues to ring.

"It might be about your mother," I say quietly.

"My mother is in the very capable hands of a private nurse she hired." He taps his finger on his knee. "I believe they went to the theater tonight and then they likely went to dinner. She's fine."

I scratch my neck. "A private nurse? She's okay, isn't she?"

"She's one of the healthiest people I know." He brushes his fingers across my cheek. "She had an anxiety attack that night, nothing more. I'm not concerned about her. I want to focus on you. What did you want to talk about?"

210

Maybe that's actually the sign that I've been waiting for. He'll understand. He has issues with his own mother. I clasp my hands together in front of me. I take a deep breath and I look right into his eyes. "My mother is suing me. She's trying to take away everything my grandmother left me."

CHAPTER THIRTY-EIGHT

Gabriel

It takes a moment for the words to sink in. Her mother is suing her. Suing.

"My grandmother is Ella Amherst. She was Ella Amherst." She wrings her small hands together. "I know you probably don't know who that is, but she was very well known. She was very successful."

"Your grandmother was Lady Amherst?"

She laughs loudly, her hand bolting to her mouth. "She started calling herself that and it stuck. She liked the way it sounded."

"Isla." I move forward on the bed. "My mother loved Lady Amherst. She had recordings, actual records, of her music. Your grandmother was gifted. I had no idea."

"We don't share the same last name." She pulls on the dainty earring in her left ear. "She never took my grandfather's name. She told me that she liked her own too much."

"You have a beautiful name," I say it because it's obviously the truth. "You inherited your grandmother's talent though. That's why you play the way you do."

"I will never be as good as her." She smooths her hand over her hair. "She was one in a million."

"As are you, Isla."

"You're too kind." She looks up at me. "We were very close. I lived with her before she died.

212

There were some issues with my mother so my grandmother was given custody of me."

"Issues?" I ask because I suspect it's much more serious than a disobedient teenage girl rebelling against her mother.

Her gaze follows my movements as I lean forward onto my right hand. She looks so angelic in this light, so fair and innocent. I've been tempted, for weeks now, to have someone delve into her background. I've craved the details of her life before she worked at the boutique but it's her story to tell, not mine to discover. If her grandmother is gone and her mother is suing her, what the fuck is her father doing?

"I toured when I was a child." She closes her eyes and shakes her head abruptly. "That sounds pompous. My mother was my manager. She booked me to perform at different places."

"Perform where?"

"Anywhere we could make a dollar or two." She taps her fingers one-by-one. "Weddings, funerals, bar mitzvahs, graduation parties, birthday parties, you name it."

"In Chicago?" I study her face. "This happened in Chicago?"

She shrugs. "It began there but she saw opportunity everywhere. We started traveling all over the world. She pulled me out of school. She married a man from Chicago just so he'd take care of my sisters I think."

"When did this end?"

"I had to repeat seventh grade." She covers her face with her hands. "I failed because I didn't know anything when I took the final exam. My grandmother stepped in then."

"Stepped in how?" I ask the question softly. "Is that when she took custody of you?"

She hesitates before she answers, her hands pulling at the blanket covering her lap. "My mother spent everything I'd earned. My grandmother came to get me one day and my mother didn't stop her."

She didn't stop her because Isla was no longer providing her with what she needed. "Where was your father in all of this?"

Her head pops up quickly, her bottom lip trembling. "I don't know him. My mother met him at a bar. She never knew his last name."

Fuck. Fuck all of these people who let this happen.

"May I have some water please?" she asks so softly. Her voice is so vulnerable that my heart aches for her. "I'm thirsty."

I nod before I pull myself up and walk out of the room, knowing that whatever I have to do, I'm going to protect her.

***

"Mr. Ryan," she begins before she hands me the empty glass. "Garrett is advising me not to settle with my mother, but I think I want to."

I brought her a full glass of water almost thirty minutes ago. Since then she's sipped at it while telling me about her mother's quest to get her greedy fucking hands on Isla's inheritance. What mother steals from her child, not once, but twice? The woman should be

214

held accountable for what she's done, not given a portion of the money intended for Isla's future.

"Tell me why you want to settle." I place the glass on the nightstand. "Where is that coming from?"

She glances at me. "When I was a little girl my mother loved me a lot. She doesn't anymore."

Jesus. Please. How can anyone mistreat her?

I can't offer her anything in response to that. My mother may not be perfect, but she loves me. I know that wholly.

"I moved to New York because one day I want to play with the Philharmonic." Her expression shifts. "My grandmother wanted that for me. I want that for me."

"I believe it will happen, Isla." I don't say the words lightly. She's determined, and beyond that, incredibly talented.

"Since I came here, my mother has been sending me things." She purses her lips together. "Letters, gifts, pictures."

"Why?"

Her brows arch. "At first I misunderstood. I thought she wanted to repair things between us. I thought she'd drop the lawsuit so we could mend our relationship."

I'll ask even though the answer is painfully obvious in her face. "That wasn't her intention, was it?"

She inches forward on the bed and I sense her need. I tug her into my lap, pulling her close to my chest, cradling her in my arms.

I feel the deep sigh that flows through her as she settles next to my chest. "She did it to try and make me feel sorry for her. She told me that any decent daughter would take care of her mother. All those things she sent me were just meant to remind me that once, a very long time ago, she loved me and I could pay to have that back."

CHAPTER THIRTY-NINE

Isla

"Have you considered studying at Juilliard?" He asks as soon as I pull the bow from the strings. I'd played three of my favorite compositions for him while I sat cross legged on the bed, wearing only his dress shirt. He's sitting in the chair nearby, a white robe open around him.

Our discussion earlier ended when I went to get my violin case so I could play for him. I know that he wanted to talk more about my fucked up relationship with my mother, but I couldn't bear it. I felt so exposed, so vulnerable that I had to retreat to the place where I feel safe. That's with my violin. It offers a comfort that nothing else can.

"I was accepted to Juilliard," I confess softly. "I was granted a full scholarship before I graduated from high school."

"So you studied there and then took a job at Liore?"

I'm pretty sure if I studied at the most prestigious music school in the country that I wouldn't be hawking expensive lingerie in his store.

"No." I cradle my instrument in my hands. "The scholarship offer was withdrawn."

"Why?" He moves from the chair to the corner of the bed in one fluid motion. "Why would that happen?"

My chest tightens. "I was suspended from high school more than once. I broke the rules."

A ghost of a grin flies over his lips before he pulls them into a thin line. "What rules did you break?"

"Name one," I say flippantly. "I broke most of them."

"You were truant?"

"Truant?" I repeat back. "You're asking if I skipped classes?"

"Yes."

"Many."

"You had bad grades?" He bends his leg at the knee. "Did you fail some of your classes?"

I stare at this cock long enough for him to tap my thigh to get my attention. "I didn't fail anything in high school. That's not a rule."

"Tell me what you did that got you into so much trouble."

I trace my fingers over the weathered wood of the violin. It was a gift from my grandmother. It had been her instrument for years before she purchased another. It's my most treasured possession.

"I was late for class a lot. I got caught. I made out with a boy on school grounds. I got caught for that too."

"Those aren't serious infractions. You lost your scholarship because of those things?" His eyes are warm, his expression understanding.

My brows rise. "I lost my scholarship when I was caught cheating. That's one of the hard and fast rules you can't break."

"You were caught cheating?" I hear the disbelief in his tone as much as I hear it in the words. "What was it, Isla? Algebra? History? Did you smuggle the answers to a test in on a piece of paper or maybe you wrote them on your hand?"

"Nothing like that," I mutter. "It was economics. It was a year after my grandmother died and I had been at the cemetery. I rushed to school for the test. I forgot my notes were in my bag. After the test the teacher searched all of our bags and he found them."

"That's extenuating circumstances, Isla."

"No, Gabriel." I set my violin down on the bed next to me. "That is cheating, according to my high school."

"You broke all these rules after she died, didn't you?"

I bite my bottom lip to hold back the tears. "I was only seventeen when she died. I had to go live with my mother for that year. Every single day was a blur. I just wanted to escape my life. I just wanted to escape all that pain."

***

"I know people in the admissions office at Juilliard." He stares at my reflection in the bathroom mirror as he adjusts his tie. "I can make a few calls today."

I'm not surprised by the offer. I anticipated it, although I admit, I thought he might do it behind my back.

"No," I say firmly as I smooth my hands over the same black dress I was wearing last night. "I can reapply if I want."

"If you reapplied, you'd be accepted, Isla." He straightens his jacket. "I promise I won't become involved unless that's something you desire."

It would be the easy track to get my life back to where I want it but it would also create a debt I don't want between us. I can take care of myself, and my life. I want, and need, for him to fully understand and support that.

"I might quit my job at the boutique soon."

That statement warrants a full turn on his part until he's facing me directly. "You're going to quit your job?"

"I've been waiting for an opening at a music school on the Upper West Side." I pull my hair up and into a ponytail, using the elastic band I keep in my purse. "I would teach violin to children."

His hands fall together in front of him. "That sounds interesting."

"It's a private school." I look past him to the mirror, realizing that my face is still flushed from when he'd licked me to orgasm after we'd woken this morning.

We'd fallen asleep holding each other after I shared the tortured confessions of my high school days. He hadn't said anything after I spoke of the pain I felt when my grandmother died, but his silence and comfort were exactly what I needed.

"This is what you want?"

I smile softly as I rake him from head-to-toe. He looks stunning, as always, dressed in a suit, freshly shaved, his hair in place. "I want all of that but I can't be late for work. Cicely will fire me and I want to have the satisfaction of seeing her face when I quit."

He chuckles. "I wasn't referring to my body, Isla. The job; the teaching job, that's what you want?"

"I want to play my violin. I want to share music with others. This is how I can do that right now."

"I'm fully behind this." He turns back towards the mirror. "It's a win-win for us."

"How so?" I dart up behind him, wrapping my arms around his chest.

He pats my hands with his. "You get to do what you enjoy and I get to breathe again knowing that you'll kccp your clothes on when you're at work."

CHAPTER FORTY

Gabriel

"Who knew dad was only worth low six figures." Caleb waves me into his office. "How much do you think I'm worth?"

"A buck ninety-nine on a good day."

"Fuck you," he shoots back with a grin. "You're funny now, too? Who the hell is this woman you're sinking your dick into? She needs a goddamn medal."

I've yet to introduce Isla formally to any of my family. She did have that awkward meeting with my mother at my office, but the moment I explain that she's Lady Amherst's granddaughter, Isla will become the apple of my mother's eye. I already know that. I saw it when my mother listened to Isla playing in the atrium that evening weeks ago.

"Have you spoken to Roman about Caterina?" I walk towards the windows. His office isn't nearly as spacious as mine and the view pales in comparison, but he's content here. His life has evolved the past few months since he married. His time here, in the building, is limited to nine-to-five, no more, often less.

"I broke his heart last night." He shifts restlessly. "I sent him the emails we exchanged with her and an image of the cashed check."

"Will he speak to us again?" I already know the answer to that. My father, although a proud man, is aware of his appeal to the younger women he courts. He knows that they're not drawn to his greying hair and sizable paunch. He may have believed otherwise before today. The fact that his fiancé took a check worth much less than I was prepared to offer is proof of her motivations.

Caterina Omari actually took our first offer, with little fanfare. I could almost hear her drooling over the phone. That problem is solved.

"He's coming into town next week." He taps out a message on his smartphone. "We'll do dinner. You can bring the woman who unearthed your personality."

"Fuck you."

"We're done." He gestures back towards the door. "I don't get to dismiss you often so I'm taking pleasure in this."

"How's Rowan?"

"Pregnant."

That pushes me to sit in the chair in front of his desk. "What?"

"You heard me old man." It's the nickname he hasn't since we were in high school. "I'm going to be a dad. Me? Wrap your mind around that."

I can't. Literally, I cannot imagine my younger brother as a father. "She's pregnant?"

"Three months pregnant." He beams. "We don't know yet if it's a boy or a girl, but I don't give a fuck what it is. I'm going to have a child, Gabriel."

I stare at him across the desk. He's only two years younger than me but every time I look at him I see the same eight-year-old kid who used to sit next to me on the stoop of the brownstone we lived in.

He'd ask me about all the constellations and I'd point them out, one-by-one, while he sat quietly listening.

Somewhere between then and now he grew up. He got married and now, he's going to be a father. He'll be a good one; an honest and protective one. He'll be remarkable.

"I'm happy for you both." I stand again.

He reaches out his hand as an offering but I ignore it. Instead I round his desk, push his chair back and pull my younger brother into a warm embrace.

***

"Isla flashed her underwear to a customer, sir." Cicely shoots Isla a look across the boutique.

"Did she now?"

She turns towards where I'm standing. "I think that's breaking a rule, sir. She's always breaking the rules."

I study the receipts for yesterday's sales. "I should punish her for that."

"Just look at her now." She nudges her elbow into my side. "Her dress is practically falling open."

I tap my finger on the front counter. "Isla's sales are still the most impressive, Cicely. Yours could stand some improvement."

She grabs hold of my forearm as she peers down at the numbers. "I have to take care of everything, sir. It's a lot to manage all the employees."

"You're having difficulty keeping everything in check?"

Her body stiffens, her hand darting to the front of her dress. "No, I didn't mean that. Isla is just a handful."

"Indeed she is."

She waits a moment before she responds. "I saw her open her dress on the security footage, sir. She just untied it and there it all was. I can show you if you want."

The fact that she hasn't fired Isla herself is evidence enough that it was a woman Isla showed her lingerie to, and not a man. "I don't need to see it. I'll speak to Isla about it."

"What's going on with her? Is there something going on between you two?"

The question irritates me enough that I turn to face her. "Why are you asking?"

Her arms cross over her chest in a defensive way. "She breaks a lot of rules and never gets in trouble."

"She has yet to break a rule that would warrant terminating her employment, Cicely," I remind her. "You've broken rules as well. You didn't do your job the morning that refuse was found in the change room. If you had, it would have been a non-issue."

"What is it about girls like her?" Her hand flies in the air behind her head. "Why do men like you always want girls like that?"

"I have no idea what other men want." I look past her to where Isla is standing. Her face lit up in a smile as she speaks to a customer. "I can tell you that Isla is not a girl. She's an incredibly complex woman and I'm honored whenever she spends time with me."

"Whatever," she mumbles as she walks away. "I seriously do not get the appeal."

CHAPTER FORTY-ONE

Isla

I scan my apartment one last time before I open the door.

"Isla." He grabs my shoulders before he leans down to kiss me softly. "You look beautiful."

He always says that. I think I could be wearing a burlap sack and a pointy hat on my head and he'd say the exact same thing. I'm not complaining. I like it. I'll never tire of it.

He, on the other hand, looks striking. He's dressed completely in black. This is one of the few times I've seen him outside his penthouse without a tie.

"This is where I live," I state the obvious out of nervousness. Of course this is where I live. I'm the one who gave him the address when he asked if he could pick me up for dinner.

I move aside as he brushes past me. "It's larger than I imagined. It's comfortable?"

"It's no penthouse overlooking Central Park," I tease. "I like it a lot though. I really like it now that my roommate has left."

"I thought she was moving out on Friday."

I thought the same until she told me that Nigel's roommate had bailed on him so she was going to move in there. It's financially the best decision for them both and as she packed up what was left of her things last night, I'd given her a huge hug and watched her walk out the door.

We'll still meet for lunch and dinners. We'll hang out sometimes but our lives are moving in different directions.

"She had an opportunity to move sooner, so she took it."

He reaches for my hands, pulling them into his. "You're trembling, Isla. What is it?"

I glance towards my bedroom. There's no reason for me to be nervous. This is what I want. It's why I stopped on my way home from work last night in a small store I had peered in night after night. I'm not doing this for him. Well, not just for him. This is for me.

"Kiss me." I perch myself up on my tiptoes. I have yet to put on my heels, or my panties, for that matter. The only thing I'm wearing is the navy blue sheath dress he's never seen me in before.

He cradles my face in his palms as he kisses me slow and deep, his delicious tongue diving into my mouth, coaxing me. I moan into the kiss as he trails his teeth over my bottom lip. This time I don't pull back when he bites me.

"What was it for?" I say breathlessly against his mouth.

"You did open your dress for a customer." His smile presses against mine. "Cicely wasn't impressed."

"I give zero fucks about Cicely. Zero."

He laughs then. The sound vibrates through me. How did I get this lucky? What did I ever do in my life to deserve the attention of this man?

"I want the things we do to be just about us." I stop to kiss him again.

He pulls me closer, his hands now wrapped lightly around my neck. "They are, Isla. Everything we ever do will just be about us."

"I bought you a gift."

His fingers run through my hair. "A gift? For me?"

I close my eyes, doubting for just a moment whether this is a good idea or not.

"Show me?" Expectation laces his words. "I want to see what it is."

"Gabriel." I press my mouth against his one more time, reveling in the sweet taste of his breath and the scent of his skin. "My bedroom is the first door on the left. Please give me five minutes. Just five and then you'll come in."

He kisses me then, with a low growl. "Five minutes, Isla. Not a minute more."

***

My heart stops for two beats when I hear the door open and the sound he makes. It's not a moan, it doesn't resemble a word. It's a slow, guttural sound that drives every ounce of desire to my core instantly.

"Jesus, Isla," he hisses as he walks into my view. "This is for me? You did this for me?"

The only light in the room are the vanilla scented candles I've placed around the space. There may be a dozen, maybe less. I lost count when I lit them with my shaky hands.

I'd pulled my dress off then, securing the black fur collar around my neck. I pulled the crop from the box I've kept it in since I bought it. I held it in my palms, imagining his strong hand wrapped around the handle as he pulls it over my skin, before he brings it down in a harsh snap.

"Isla," he says my name softly as he takes off his jacket, tossing it on a chair near the bed. "I've never seen anything more beautiful than this."

My body is completely on display. My thighs spread not more than a few inches, my pussy wet, wanting, aching for him.

He rolls up the sleeves of his shirt, his eyes never leaving mine.

I whimper faintly when he lowers one knee to the bed as he scoops up the handcuffs I'd left on the nightstand. He kisses a trail of soft bites up my right arm before he closes the cuff around my wrist. He wraps them around the post of my headboard before a soft line of kisses dot my left arm. When I'm finally bound he leans down. His index finger loops through the metal ring on the front of the collar. He pulls it up, my neck slowly bending with the movement as he pulls me into his waiting kiss.

"Haze, Isla."

"Haze," I repeat.

He moves back to look at me. His eyes focused solely on my face. "You don't know what you do to me. You can't understand what this means to me."

I nod as I bite my bottom lip, stalling the emotion that I'm feeling. "Please, sir."

His hand catches the handle of the crop. He brings it up into my view. His other hand stroking its length before it settles on the leather tongue at the top.

I moan the moment he lowers it to my cheek. He pulls it along, the leather warm and hard. "Slow tonight, beautiful Isla. We'll go slow."

I nod in response, not even sure that there are words I can form.

The leather glides along my chin, down my neck and across my chest. I stare up and into his face, watching the subtle nuances as his brows lift when the leather circles my nipple. I'm so aroused that they ache, they ache already and he has barely touched them.

I cry out when he slaps my right nipple with the leather. The pain only silenced by the pleasure in his breathing. He moans slightly. It's so soft that if there was any rustling in the room beyond the movement of his shirt as he reaches forward, I'd miss it. It would be lost.

My eyes close, heavy with both want and need. I listen more intently. I hear his shoes as they shift on the hardwood floors, the sound of my labored breathing woven into the steady and increasing beats of my heart.

I scream when the leather slaps my left nipple, not once, not twice, but again and again.

His lips are on me then, his breath in my mouth, his tongue on mine. "I adore you, Isla. I adore you."

I nod again. This time, knowing that if I tried to speak it would be a twisted mess of emotions I'm not ready to share.

I feel the soft touch of his hand on my hip as he pushes me to my side. I help, sliding my body over, my wrists still cuffed above my head.

The leather glides down my skin, stopping at the top of my ass. He circles it over and over again in the center of my back. The sensation hypnotic, relaxing, so calming.

"Gabriel," I whisper his name against my lips as I open my eyes. He's behind me. I can see the faint movement of his shirt as his forearm circles into view again, and then again, and yet again.

I moan when the leather inches down across my ass, circling a small space. I push back when it slaps me, my body craving more. I rub my thighs together, desperate for anything that will stimulate my clit enough for me to get off.

He growls his disapproval, approval, something into the air as the leather slaps me again, time and again.

I'm on my back now, the crop being pulled along my belly to the place that I crave. He inches my legs apart with the tip. I acquiesce, letting my thighs drop to the bed.

The leather glides over my folds slowly; it's so painfully slow that I whimper aloud as I close my eyes. "I want to come."

"You will."

It's right then that he gives me what I want. The harsh and tight leather circles that spot. He hones in on my clit and I lift my hips from the bed as he touches me, in the most intimate way, with a small piece of leather and only his words.

"Your cunt is so beautiful. I love the way it tastes. I love the way you grip my cock when you come. I'm going to fuck you so hard."

"Please, Gabriel," I beg for release. I want the sting of the pain. I want to know what it's like to feel that.

It moves and I scream out of sheer desperation. My reward is a sharp snap of the leather against my inner thigh and then another and then just as I open my eyes, I feel his weight on the bed. Everything shifts; each sound becomes louder, each fragrance stronger, my body's own need to come is all that I can feel and think about.

I watch as he pulls a condom from his pocket before he sheaths his thick cock. He leans forward, pulling his shirttails out of the way as he pushes into me balls deep, pulling my right leg up into his arm. The sensation is so intense that I weep as I arch my ass of the bed.

"So fucking good." The words spill from his lips into mine as he kisses me hard, fucking me even harder. I come fast. It's so fast that it spurs him on even more.

"I will never get enough of this." The words fall from his lips as he grinds himself into me. "I will never get enough of you."
I kiss him, wanting everything he can give to me and when his body shakes as he comes, only one word fills the room. Isla. Isla. Isla.

CHAPTER FORTY-TWO

Gabriel

I open my eyes, immediately aware that I've slept in a bed that doesn't belong to me. I'm also instantly, and gratefully aware, that Isla is next to me. I feel her lush body pressed against mine. The curve of her ass is visible when I glance down.

I'd fucked her twice. Once when she was cuffed to the bed and then again hours later after she'd taken my cock between her lips. She was on her knees on the floor next to the bed, the soft collar still wrapped around her neck as she swallowed every inch of my cock, urging me to come in her mouth.

I wanted it. I fucking wanted it so badly but I wanted to be inside her more and when I guided her back onto my lap, she'd hesitated. I knew what it meant. I was ready. I motioned for her to grab the condom I'd pulled out of the pocket of my pants.

She'd sheathed me herself, taking care to cover me tenderly, before she inched back into my lap and lowered her slick cunt over me. It was incredible, the angle, the sensations, the sight of her tits bouncing as she rode me hard.

Her lips were swollen, her body misted and when she came that time, she'd cursed. The words driving me mad, mad enough to circle her waist with my arm so I could drive my cock up and inside of her until I came. I'd dropped onto my back then, pulling her with me.

234

She's ruined me. I felt it for weeks now. I've ignored it all but now I feel it in every part of me. I'll never get over this.

"We haven't had dinner." She pushes her back into my chest. "Are you hungry, Gabriel?"

No, it's not hunger. I'm in love. I think I'm in love. I have no bearing for that but this feels like love.

I wrap my arms around her, nestling my face in the softness of her hair. "I can cook something. What do you have to eat?"

"Mustard."

I laugh when I realize she's not going to say another thing. "You only have mustard?"

"It's the fancy one." She kicks her feet to move the blankets. "You probably eat it by the truckload. You know what I'm talking about."

I pull her closer. "Yellow mustard, Isla?"

"Ha," she says loudly. "You know that's not it. It's the fancy one."

"Grey Poupon?"

"I have that," she says with a horrible English accent. "You're welcome to eat it by the spoon if you like."

I cringe. "You don't eat it by the spoonful, do you?"

"I hate mustard." She rolls over, pulling her hand along her face to move her hair. "It was Cassia's, my roommate's. It's not even mine."

"What would you like to eat? I can order something in."

"Pizza." She taps my chest with both her hands. "Let's have pizza."

***

"Why haven't you told anyone?" She chews the last bite of her slice. "Have you considered talking to your mom about it?"

I've never thought about talking to anyone about it, especially my mother. It's a subject that I've kept hidden inside of me for most of my life. At the very least, since I was a teenager when I sensed what was happening.

"My mother's affairs are her own." I wince at my own choice of words. "I don't know what good would come of it if I confront her."

"You just told me that you know, for a fact, that she cheated on your dad with at least two men."

"I also know, for a fact that my father cheated on my mother with as many, if not more women."

She swipes a paper napkin across her lips. "It's really fucked up. They made vows. They promised one another."

"There was always a lot of discontent in their marriage," I say softly. "They were always arguing. There was so much back and forth that it was actually a relief when they decided to divorce."

She leans back against the headboard of her bed. "Do you ever think they regret it? Do you think they still care about each other at all?"

I love this part of her. It's hopeful and naïve. She may have lived through many difficult things within her own family but she's never been touched by the volatility of a relationship like the one my parents have.

"I think my mother still loves Roman, my father, in a sense," I say coolly. "There's still something there. She was very upset when he got engaged."

"I read that his fiancé called it off." She pushes the pizza box towards me. "You should eat more."

"I'm full." I slam the box shut.

"If I ever get married, I want it to be forever." She looks across the room at the candles which I'd blown out hours ago when she first fell asleep. "I know that's silly to say, but it's my dream. It's one of my dreams."

I lean forward to graze my lips across her bare knee. "It's not silly if that's your dream, Isla."

She pinches the bridge of her nose, her eyes shuttering for a moment. "I wanted the crop to be for just you and me. The collar I was wearing too."

I swallow back my emotions. "I understand."

"I know there are others." She closes her eyes again. "I didn't want to be just one of them."

"There are no other women in my life." I rest my chin against her knee. "You could never be like anyone else."

She glides her hand over my forehead. "Thank you for tonight. I want more."

"We'll do whatever you wish, Isla, whenever you wish."

Her hand stops on my cheek. "Was it special, Gabriel? Did it feel as special to you as it did to me?"

"It was everything to me. Everything," I say before I kiss her.

CHAPTER FORTY-THREE

Isla

"I quit." That felt better than I ever imagined it would.

"Sure."

No, just no. Fight me on this Cicely. Get mad. Give me something. Throw me a fucking bone.

"Sure?" I round the counter so I'm facing her directly. "What do you mean?"

She shrugs her orange fabric colored shoulder. "You quit. I get it."

I stomp my foot. This isn't happening. I need some satisfaction here. "You're not upset at all?"

"Are you asking if I'm going to miss you, Isla?"

I'm not asking that, am I?

She looks down at a stack of papers in front of her. I follow the movement as her shaking hands scatter the papers about before she pulls them back into a pile.

"What's wrong?" I reach forward and grab her wrists. "Tell me what's going on."

Her shoulders stiffen. "I saw Lance last night."

"Lance?" I try to remember if she ever mentioned a Lance before. No, there's no way. I'm sure I would remember that. "Who is Lance?"

"You know who he is."

Apparently she did mention Lance and I was too awestruck by her choice of wardrobe that day that I zoned out. I'm going to go for the obvious. "Is he the man you loved?"

She nods quickly. "He came to see me. We went for dinner."

Somehow we've become confidantes since I quit my job twenty seconds ago. "Did it go well?"

I'm greeted with a loud sniffle. "He wants to get back together."

"That's good?" I ask cautiously. "It's good, right?"

"He's a secretary, Isla," she hisses. "He works for Alec Hughes as his secretary."

If I knew who Alec Hughes is that might make this easier to understand. I'll take a random shot in the dark. The only Hughes I've ever heard of is the man who owns the company that Cassia is interning at. "Hughes Enterprises? Lance works there?"

"Don't sound so impressed."

"I'm not."

Her head bolts up. "So you agree with me? You wouldn't date a man who is a secretary either, would you?"

"I once dated a guy who cleaned windshields at red lights for tips, Cicely. I'm not the best judge."

She smiles. She actually smiles. "My parents think it's ridiculous. They want me to be with someone like Mr. Foster."

He's taken. Hands-off.

"Why do you give a fuck what your parents think? They're not dating him."

"They have a reputation. They don't want it sullied by someone like Lance," she says every single one of those words with a straight face.

"Sullied? Do your parents live in this century, Cicely?"

Another smile, this one brighter. "I don't want to disappoint them, Isla."

I tap her on the chest. "This is what you worry about. It's your heart, Cicely. You love this guy, don't you?"

"I love him more than anything."

"Don't lose him. Sully whatever you need to in order to keep him."

She nods, straightening the legs of her orange pantsuit. "I'll take your advice but I'm still not going to miss you."

"I won't miss you either." I pull her into a tight hug. "I won't miss you at all."

***

"You decided to go ahead and settle with your mother?" Gabriel cocks a dark winged brow. "You feel confident that's the best decision for you."

"I do." I'd gone to Garrett's office after work today. As much as I had wanted to quit on the spot yesterday, I did give Cicely a full two weeks' notice. I don't want to leave her in a bind and I won't start working at the music school until a week after that.

My plan now is to polish my craft so that when I do land an audition with Juilliard, I'll be prepared and I'll have the funds in place to pay for my own tuition.

240

"I'm happy for you then, Isla."

I don't push him on whether he believes it's the best decision because it's not his life. It's mine and putting the drama with my mother behind me will give me the emotional freedom I need to finally move forward without all this weighing me down.

"I need a financial advisor." I look across the table at him. "Can you offer any suggestions?"

A grin tugs at the corners of his mouth. "I have several I'd highly recommend. I'll put you in touch with them and then you can decide the right fit for your needs."

"That's very helpful."

He brings the glass of ice water to his lips. He drinks it slowly, all the while watching me over the rim. "I will help you in any way I can. You need only ask and I'll be right there. I'm always available for you."

"Can we talk about the other night?"

He shifts slightly in his chair, his eyes darting around the almost empty restaurant. "Yes, of course. What would you like to talk about?"

"You seem uncomfortable." I look towards the door. "We can go to another place if you prefer."

He shakes his head slightly from side-to-side. "This is fine. I've never been here. I don't generally wander into this part of the city."

"I don't either," I confess. "A customer who lives in the neighborhood said this place was fantastic."

He moves again. This time his hand scoops up his smartphone from the table. He scans the screen

before he places it back down. It's not an act of
curiosity. He's nervous, really, really nervous.

"Haze."

That brings another smile to his lips. A soft
one. "You use your safeword at the most interesting
times, Isla. What's going on?"

"Did I take you away from something
important when I asked you to meet me here?"

"No," he answers quickly. "Not at all."

I don't know where to take the conversation
from here. I can't push if I have no idea what's
troubling him. He runs a huge fashion conglomerate. I
imagine that he has a mountain of problems weighing
him down on any given day.

"Tell me where haze comes from?" He
motions to the server. "I'm going to need a drink after
all."

I sit quietly while he orders a glass of red
wine. I don't say anything while he types a message
on his phone until the drink arrives.

"It came from you."

"What came from me?" he asks quietly. "Haze
came from me?"

I reach forward to pull the wine glass towards
me. I tip it back, swallowing a mouthful of the rich,
red liquid. "Yes, it came from you."

He looks at me intently, his eyes studying
every curve of my lips before they move to my eyes.
"Explain, Isla."

"It's silly." I sip more of the wine, enjoying
the warmth it provides in not only my throat but my
entire body. "It's going to sound so stupid."

"There is nothing that you could ever say to me that would sound stupid." He raps his fingers on the top of the wooden table. "Tell me."

"I'm not sure why I applied at the boutique. I mean I wanted a job and when I was walking past one day there was a sign in the window. It said that there were jobs, so I walked in."

"I recall Cicely posting a notice on the window."

"I spoke to Wallis that day. She hired me on the spot after I filled out the application. I started the day after that."

"It was a quick process." He glides the glass back towards him, taking a small gulp before he pushes it back to me.

"I got up every day and went there. I did my job. I came home and every day I would stop at the deli two blocks up from my place and buy a turkey sandwich."

"A turkey sandwich with no mustard?"

"Yes, no mustard." I smile. "Then you came into the store that day. I swear that when I turned around and looked up at you, there was this glow around you."

His hands rest on the table. "Tell me more."

I feel a rush of embarrassment. "I wanted to kiss you. I really wanted to kiss you in your office that day you reprimanded me for inviting myself there."

"The day you said you'd come for a private lingerie show?"

"It was more of a private fuck me please party, but that's semantics."

He laughs loudly, his head falling back. "The truth finally comes out."

"That's part of it," I say softly. "That's just the beginning."

CHAPTER FORTY-FOUR

Gabriel

"Tell me the ending, Isla."

She looks at the wine glass, her fingers inching towards it, before she pulls them back with a faint shake of her head. "We obviously didn't kiss that day and then I thought you were hooking up with Cicely."

"That's unfortunate," I quip.

"She seriously made it sound like you were dating." She rolls her big blue eyes. "I bought into that. I totally believed she was your type."

"You are my only type." I lean back in my chair, feeling much less anxious than I did ten minutes ago.

She dips her chin down but not before I see the faint rush of pink that takes over her cheeks as she blushes.

"I was excited when I saw you at the charity event at the symphony." She pushes her hair back over her left shoulder, a few strands clinging to the fabric of her black dress. "You look amazing in a tuxedo, by the way."

I smile, not wanting to interrupt her.

"I've kissed men before," she admits with a tilt of her hand in the air. "I mean of course I have, but it was different when you kissed me in your car."

"Different in what way?" My curiosity, when it comes to Isla, is an uncontainable beast.

245

"Intense, powerful, the connection between us felt basic and primal."

"It was that way for me as well." I adjust my legs, crossing them in a thinly veiled attempt to mask my growing erection. Kissing Isla is almost as sensual as licking her cunt or fucking her. It's a treasure of flavors and sensations. It's something I could do for hours.

"Please don't think I'm foolish." Her voice cracks with the words. "I'm not a foolish person."

"You're an incredibly special person. The most special person I know. I don't consider you foolish at all."

She nods as she leans back in her chair. "I write poetry. I used to write poetry."

The admission pushes me back as well. Not only physically in my chair, but on an emotional level as well. I don't want to derail her right now, but I'm on the edge of understanding so much. I don't want to lose that.

She tilts her body to the left, pulling up her bag. It's a larger purse than I've seen her with before. It's black, tattered and it's obvious she's had it for years. "I brought my poetry with me."

Her small hand dives into the bag and pulls out a blue notepad. The pages are askew, single papers jutting out from the sides. It's a complicated mess.

"I wrote my first poem the day after my grandmother died."

She opens the pages slowly. Her hands delicately smoothing over the paper. "Would you like to read it?"

I'd love nothing more. "Yes."

Tears fill her eyes, making the irises more vibrant than they normally are. She's so fragile and strong and such an intricate, incredible person.

"It's called Haze."

I try to drop my eyes to the paper but as I look at the tears streaming down her face, I understand. "How many poems have you written, Isla?"

"Hundreds."

"Tell me the name of the second poem you wrote."

She sobs quietly. "Haze."

I swallow hard. "The third?"

"Haze."

"When did you write the last poem, Isla?"

"Two nights before my birthday."

I stop there out of my own selfish need to read her words. I rest my forehead on my hand, my elbow propped on the table as I read the tortured words of a young woman desperately alone in the world.

I am alone in this haze called life.

Every single day is a haze.

What does it feel like to live beyond the haze.

Haze…

Repeated again and again.

"This is your safeword?"

"I knew I'd never say it when I'm with you." She pulls in a deep breath. "You're supposed to pick something you know you wouldn't say when you're with that person."

I nod as I stare into her face.

"The haze disappeared when you kissed me."

CHAPTER FORTY-FIVE

Isla

The moment I step out of the washroom and back into the almost vacant restaurant I know something is wrong. I'd only gone in there to fix my make-up after I'd sobbed in front of Gabriel. I knew I'd show him my poetry tonight. It's not publication worthy, and I don't intend to ever show it to another person, but it's part of my relationship with him, so it was a gift I had to share.

His head is bowed as he talks on his phone. His eyes shielded to me by his hand as he cups it over his brow. He's impatient with the person on the other end, scolding them with his tone, if not his words, which I'm too far away to hear.

I glance at the table, realizing that approaching it now, would only interrupt him. It has to be business. He must be dealing with something beyond my scope of understanding. I don't run a company. I can't imagine ever doing that.

My passion is music and now that my life is settled, it's where my time and energy will be spent.

I walk towards the bar, which is dotted with a handful of people, sitting on stools. I smile at the bartender as I order another glass of wine to share with Gabriel.

The drink will help calm my nerves, and there's something intimate in sharing a glass with him.

"Do we know each other?" A female voice pulls at me from the left. "Isla, is that you?"

I turn quickly when I realize it's Tiffany, a customer, from the boutique. "Tiffany, how are you?"

She pulls me into a quick embrace. "I'm well. I'm here to grab a quick drink with a friend. Do you want to join us?"

"I'm here with someone." I don't gesture towards the table. Gabriel and I haven't made our relationship public yet. I'm not sure if that matters to him, but it's not my place to announce it to the world. Besides, I like having him like this, just for me.

"There's my friend now." She looks around me towards a woman who just walked through the door. She's tall, beautiful, her hair spiky and black.

"Sage." Tiffany stretches her hand out to the woman. "This is Isla."

The woman stops short of where we're standing, her gaze raking me from head-to-toe before a sly smile takes over her mouth. "I know Isla, or technically, I've seen Isla before."

"At the Liore boutique?" Tiffany asks. "It's where I met her too."

"It wasn't there." Sage gestures towards the door. "It was just down the street from here. I saw you at Skyn."

My hand darts up to cover my chest even though the dress I'm wearing does that for me. "You saw me at Skyn?"

"Well, fuck me…" her voice trails as her eyes scan the restaurant. "You're not here with Gabriel, are you?"

I glance back to where he's still seated, his head bowed in a deep conversation. "You know Gabriel?"

She laughs then. It's not sweet or filled with any notes of enjoyment. It's dark, almost sinister. "Do I know Gabriel?"

The answer is clear. He's fucked her.

"That's the Gabriel you did all that fucked up shit with?" Tiffany giggles. "He's the one? You're not talking about Gabriel Foster, are you?"

I pull in a ragged breath. "I should go."

"You should stay so you can tell me how the fuck he found you." Sage's hand wraps around my wrist. "He picked you out in the club but then you dropped your bag and the night went straight to hell."

"He picked me out?" I ask, my voice a clear reflection of my emotions. It's shaky, quiet, confused.

"I actually had a friend all primed for him that night." She snaps her fingers in front of my face. "Then, boom, he spots you shaking your pretty little ass on the dance floor and he decides you're the one."

"The one?" I stare at her face.

"He was there trolling for a fuck and apparently you're his type."

"Isla." His voice cracks through the space.

I turn towards him but he's already next to me. "Sage, keep your fucking mouth shut."

"Oh Christ, Gabriel." She pushes his shoulder. "You already told her all this, no? What I want to know is how did you track her down?"

"We're leaving." His hand is on the small of my back. "Isla, now."

250

"He gets off on that, Isla," Sage calls after us. "Big, bossy Gabriel."

I don't hear anything else she says as we brush past the table and I pick up my poetry, shoving it back into my bag.

CHAPTER FORTY-SIX

Gabriel

She looks so small and breakable sitting in the car as she stares out the window. She hasn't said a word to me since we left the restaurant. I haven't spoken either. I'm not sure what words I can say that will wash away the pain she's feeling.

She poured everything out to me and less than an hour later, her heart was there on the floor of that dingy pub with Sage standing over it in victory.

I admit I was fearful when she'd called me earlier and asked me to meet her there. It was so close to Skyn. Much too close for my comfort but then she started telling me about her poetry and what she felt when we kissed and everything fell away.

I was ready to take her home as soon as she returned from the washroom but then Caleb called. One of our designers had quit in a huff after hearing through the grapevine about the Dante Castro debacle. I'd coached Caleb on what to say, word-for-word so he could repair the damage. I didn't want to handle it. I'd pushed it onto him so I could take care of Isla and in my haste to do that I didn't notice Sage's approach. I didn't see her walk up to Isla. By the time I did look up, the damage had been done.

"What did she mean when she said you picked me?" Her eyes stay trained on the window. "Did you pick her too?"

I watch as her hands fist around her bag, pulling it close to her chest, protecting not only its contents, but her heart. "Once, a lifetime ago, I had some encounters with her, yes."

Her shoulders tense. "At the hotel that you took me to?"

"No," I answer quickly, my eyes focused on her hands. "A cheap place by the club."

"She said you saw me at Skyn." Her voice cracks but she restores it in the next breath. "You were there the night I was?"

"Yes," I admit. "I went there that night."

Her gaze falls to her lap. "I talked about the club. You didn't tell me you saw me there."

I ache to reach over to touch her. I can't stand this distance. I can't breathe knowing she's upset with me. "You spoke about the club. You told me it was something you wanted to forget. You were humiliated by the experience. I didn't want to remind you of that."

"That's not fair." Her finger darts into the air before she pulls it back. "You should have told me you were there."

"I should have but I caused that embarrassment. I was the one who requested that you be removed from the club. I actually insisted on it. I wanted to protect you, Isla."

She shakes her head. "That makes no sense, Gabriel. She said you chose me."

I rake both hands through my hair. "I went to the club that night because I wanted to fuck you, Isla. You had been in my office the day before. I'd been up all night aching, wanting. I had to get you out of my mind, so I went there."

Her head shifts slightly, but her eyes don't move from her lap.

"Sage had someone she thought I'd like but I felt nothing when I looked at her. Then I saw you. I didn't know it was you. All I knew was that it was a woman with the most beautiful body I'd ever seen. She moved unlike any woman I'd ever known. The attraction was immediate and intense. It was exactly what I felt when I walked into the boutique and saw you the day before. Everything around me disappeared at the club that night and then you turned and I saw your face."

"You told them to throw me out?"

"Yes and then I watched them do it," I confess. "I saw what happened. I saw how humiliated you were. I wanted to go to you, hold you. I wanted to take you home."

"That's why you kissed me before my birthday in this car." Her hand slaps the seat of the car. "It's because you knew I liked those things. You knew I wanted to be handcuffed."

Jesus, please. Please don't let this steal her from me.

I move to her then, because I can't stand the pain she's in. I wrap my arm around her. She doesn't resist. "I kissed you because I wanted to. I kissed you because I have never wanted to kiss a woman more."

She turns then, her eyes a stormy shade of blue that pierce into me. "No. You kissed me because you knew I liked to be handcuffed. You saw them on the club floor, didn't you?"

I reach for her chin, cupping it in my palm. I tilt her head back. "If I never cuff you to another bed, or draw a crop across your skin again, it won't change how I feel about you. That is not what this is. I love you, Isla. I love you."

CHAPTER FORTY-SEVEN

Isla

I rest my head on his shoulder. I'm not mad that he was at the club that night. I was there too, for the exact reason he was. I wanted to fuck someone. I wanted to forget things. We ended up in the same place, under very different circumstances, but it brought us together.

"Would you have told me, Gabriel?" I look up at his face. "Do you think that you would have ever told me?"

"I would have tonight." He traces his finger over my forehead. "I hated that restaurant. It was too close to the club. I knew there was a chance someone would walk in. I also knew the chances were slim that they'd say something but the secret was suffocating me. I intended to tell you."

"Did you see me talking to the dentist?" I drop my gaze back to my lap. "I was talking to a dentist that night."

"You were talking to an asshole," he corrects me. "When I saw you turn and I knew it was you, I almost tore you away from him myself."

His arms tighten around me. "What would have happened to me that night if you weren't there?"

He rests his head against mine, his lips pressing on my forehead. "I think about that sometimes but the thoughts that it provokes terrify me. I'd go to the ends of the earth to protect you."

256

I know that he would. I saw it tonight, in the way he looked at me. I heard it when he told me he loved me.

"I need you to know that when you left the club that night, I did as well." His voice is deep and gruff. "I went home. I thought about you the entire night."

My heart stutters for a beat. "Have you been back there since?"

I know the answer isn't my business. I shouldn't care if he went back the next night or any night after that. I should only care that he wants to be with me now, yet, I can't help it.

"I don't have any intention of ever going back to the club or that hotel room."

That's an extra assurance I never would have expected. "I'm scared to be too hopeful. I don't want to feel things and then have it taken away."

He tugs me into his lap, just as he did the first night he kissed me here. He cradles my face in his palms, his dark eyes pulling me in. "If this ends, I will break into two pieces. I will fight for this. I will do whatever I need to in order to help you understand that I cherish you, Isla. You tell me what you need, and I will do that for you."

I run my finger along his brows, first the left and then the right. His face is so strong, so masculine. It's beautiful, if a man can be that. "How is it possible that you love me?"

His body shudders as he swallows. "It's impossible for me not to."

"Gabriel." I lean forward to rest my lips over his. "Don't ever stop."

***

"I should have been the one spanking you," I say breathlessly into his chest. "I didn't deserve that."

"You did." His voice is deep, husky and still filled with want. "Tonight it was a reward. I saw how wet it made you, Isla. Don't try and argue that point with me or I'll take you back over my knee."

He never technically had me over his knee in the first place.

After we got back to his penthouse, we'd sat in a chair in the living room, kissing and talking for hours. I'd asked more questions about the club and he'd answered each honestly. He helped me understand his drive to go there and the hole it had been filling within him.

I never belonged there. The scope of my experience didn't measure anywhere near his, but that night, when he saw me trying desperately to find a man to help tame my desires, he'd felt an unexplainable pull towards me.

He told me that he tried to fight it for weeks after that, but then on my birthday, when he tasted me for the first time, he lost all sight and memory of anyone else.

I believe him. I trust him. I know it's true because it's what I feel too.

He carried me to his bed after that, undressing me then. He'd licked me, and touched me, and when I tried to control his fingers on my flesh, he'd slapped my ass, over and over, all while he said my name woven into declaration of his love.

I reach down, stroking my hand over his cock. It's so long, thick. It's as beautiful and striking as he is.

"Fuck me, Gabriel," I whisper as I slide my body over his. "I want you to fuck me."

"Jesus, Isla," he hisses, his eyes closing with the words. His hands roam down my back, to my ass.

I move slightly, skimming my breasts over his chest before I kiss him, deeply, passionately.

"There are condoms in the nightstand." His arm circles my waist as he moves to the left.

I fight him, pulling him back, quieting him. "Please, just don't move."

His breathing slows as I inch back to glide my pussy over the entire length of his erection before I reach down to grab the thick root of his cock in my hand.

"Like this." I curve my body back. "Just like this. Just us."

He moans loudly as the first inch of his cock enters me, skin-on-skin, no barriers.

"You're sure." He halts my movements with both of his hands on my hips. "Isla, tell me. Tell me you're sure."

"I love you," I whisper the words into his trembling lips as I lean back, push down, and take every inch of him inside of me.

CHAPTER FORTY-EIGHT

Six Months Later

Gabriel

"I've never been more proud of you than I am right now, Isla."

She turns on her heel and pulls on my tie, tugging my head down to meet hers before she crushes her beautiful mouth into mine. The kiss is fevered, lush and deep. "It's been so long since you've fucked me. Will you fuck me now?"

"We're in the middle of Central Park." I gesture around us as I glide my hands along her back, over the thin fabric of her dress. "I fucked you last night. What's gotten into you?"

"You." She taps her hand over my chest, smoothing the tie back into place. "Tonight, after work, will you fuck me in the swing?"

The swing had been a gift. I wanted it there, in the extra bedroom waiting for us the day she moved in two months ago. I'd fucked her in it, as she moved back and forth, giving herself wholly to me, as she does each and every time we're together intimately. She's as demanding as me. She loves my body, craves it, and each and every time she touches me with the unmistakable nuance of desire, I give in.

We've experimented more. She's been responsive at times, less at others, and through it all we've found exactly what works for us. Implements complement our intimacy, but they never define it.

"Tonight, after work, I'm going to ask you to marry me, Isla."

Her eyes tear, uncontrollably. Her mouth forms a small 'o.' She doesn't make a sound, She doesn't move at the approaching chime of a bicycle bell or the loud screams of children as they come racing down the paved path towards us. Time stops.

Six hours from now or this minute won't change the course of the rest of our lives. We're not typical, we're far from ordinary. Our love story is unique as the woman standing in front of me.

The same woman who was accepted into Juilliard two hours ago because of her immense and undeniable talent. She'll begin her studies in the fall, just as the spring lines at our boutiques are launched.

One day, when we've been married for a time, I'll go to the concert hall with my mother and I'll hear my wife play with the Philharmonic. I know it will happen. I'll have seasons' tickets and I'll enjoy each performance more than the last. I will fulfill each of her dreams and if I can't, I will stand next to her as she does it herself.

I scoop the small jewelry box into my hand as I pull it from the pocket of my jacket. I slide down to one knee.

"Marry me, beautiful, Isla. Let me love you every day for the rest of my life."

She's on her knees in an instant, her blonde hair blowing in the wind, her blue eyes still lost beneath a veil of tears. "Yes, yes."

I slide the pear shaped diamond onto her finger, kissing it after it's settled. "You have changed every part of my life. I wasn't alive until I met you."

"Me too." She nods, her eyes glued to the ring. "You changed everything, Gabriel. You gave me my life back. You took me out of the haze."

EPILOGUE

One Year Later

Gabriel

"We need to hurry if we're going to make it to Zeek's birthday party on time." She stretches out on the bed. "You bought him a gift, didn't you, Gabriel?"

"Three gifts. I couldn't choose one. Why am I the only one getting dressed?" I pull a black sweater over my head before I finish zipping my jeans. "You're not going to the party nude, are you, Mrs. Foster?"

She looks at me under heavy lidded eyes. She'd been napping before I walked into the bedroom and woke her with a kiss. I wanted more. I always want more but I'd made love to her this morning when I first woke. It was slow, tender and perfect.

"I have a dress picked out." She points to the closet. "It's the blue one from Arilia that you gave me for my birthday."

It's the dress I'd seen her wearing in the photograph on her phone shortly after we'd met. I had gone to the boutique the next day and had taken it, guessing her size. I'd kept it here, in our apartment for months until I gave it to her on her twenty-second birthday. She was touched. She's worn it often since, even now that it's not fitting as it once did.

263

"Are you going to tell your mother today?" She slides her legs to the side of the bed. "I think we should wait. Today is for Caleb and Rowan. Their little boy is having his first birthday."

"We'll wait," I agree as I kneel on the floor in front of her. "We can tell her in a few days, or next week."

"Tomorrow," she counters with a kiss to my forehead. "Can we tell her tomorrow?"

"She's going to be as excited as the day you were accepted to Juilliard and the day of our wedding."

That day had been the best of my life. It was a simple wedding, at Isla's request, here in our penthouse. It was my family, some of my friends, and her friends, Cassia and Nigel. She'd worn a dress my mother helped design and as she said her vows to me, I cried. The words were so tender and giving.

"She'll be happy about it, yes?" Her finger traces over my left eyebrow. "I want her to be as happy as we are."

I place both my hands on the bed, next to her naked thighs. I lean forward resting my lips over her small, swollen belly. "My mother will love that we are naming our daughter, Ella Gianna Foster."

She lowers her hands to my hair, stroking it gently as I kiss her stomach. "We will have her in only four months. I'll be a mom in four months." "I'll be a dad," I whisper into her skin. "I'll have everything any man can ever want and I'll never, ever let it go."

THANK YOU

Thank you for purchasing my book. I can't even begin to put to words what it means to me. If you enjoyed it, please remember to write a review for it. Let me know your thoughts! I want to keep my readers happy.

For more information on new series and standalones, please visit my website, www.deborahbladon.com. There are book trailers and other goodies to check out.

If you want to chat with me personally, please LIKE my page on Facebook. I love connecting with all of my readers because without you, none of this would be possible.
www.facebook.com/authordeborahbladon

Thank you, for everything.

Preview of TORN

The Standalone

Featuring Asher Foster

"Are they low enough?"

"Pull them up." I wave my arm in the air towards one of the three female assistants he walked in with. "I need them higher."

He pushes their eager hands away as he adjusts the waistband of his button-fly jeans. I'd told him to strip down to just his pants as soon as he stepped foot into my studio. He had done that effortlessly. His hands tugging the white sweater he was wearing over his head to reveal a toned chest and stomach covered by the expected tattoos.

I'd walked closer to ask him to remove the bracelets and necklaces he had on. His eyes had been glued to mine the entire time.

I admit he's much more attractive than most of the men who traipse through here. His hair may be a tousled mess of brown but his eyes more than make up for that. They're framed by long lashes, the irises a shade of chestnut I haven't seen before.

It's no surprise that he warrants the attention he does in the media.

Asher Foster has the number one song in the country right now. On top of that, he wrote it. I listened to it on my phone before he arrived. It's moody, soulful and surprisingly brilliant.

I look through the lens of my camera. "I need that light moved to the left."

My assistant, Remy, darts into action. She pulls it over just a touch. I'd be lost without her, especially right now, given that the small space is filled with at least ten people, all part of the entourage that arrived with the Asher.

I take another glance. It's almost perfect save for the fact that when I asked him to show me some skin, he took it to a level that's bordering on obscene.

I step around the tripod and walk back towards where he's standing in front of a pale, grey canvas hung from the ceiling.

I point towards his jeans. "You can button those back up."

He looks down. "I thought you wanted me almost naked."

He's taller than I am, but only by an inch or two. It helps that I'm wearing boots with heels today. I wouldn't have chosen this short of a skirt if I'd have known that he'd be here. I try my best to always look professional but when it's over 100 degrees outside, you have to make concessions. I'm thankful I at least took the time this morning to wash and sweep my curly brown hair up so it looks controllable.

I've already established myself as the go-to photographer for celebrities in New York City. Granted, it only constitutes part of my business, but it's the most lucrative part. I'm making enough off this shoot today to pay my rent for both the studio and my apartment for the next two months.

"It was my understanding that the photograph needed to be tasteful."

"You don't think this is tasteful." There's a low growl to his voice. "Tell me what's not tasteful about it."

The room may be milling with people, but his focus is entirely on me. I've felt that since he walked in. I imagine he's used to women taking him up on everything he offers to them. There's no denying it's tempting. I only need to look down at the top of his cock visible through the opening of his jeans to know that the man is very comfortable with his body.

"I'd prefer if you buttoned your jeans up."

"Why?" His eyes darken. "Tell me what you don't like about the way I look."

There's no way in hell this man needs his ego stroked. If that's what fuels his fire he need only turn around to where every single woman in the room, including Remy, is standing with their lips at the ready.

I've always been mildly curious about why so many women are drawn towards musicians. I don't have to wonder anymore. His confidence is undeniable but it hasn't crossed the line to cocky yet. He's just the right balance of rawness mixed with blatant aggression.

"I think I look good." He playfully nods towards his groin. "You think I look good too, don't you, Falon?"

I look around the room before I rest my hand against his shoulder and lean in just a touch. "As impressive as your dick is, I don't want it in my pictures."

Coming 2016

Preview of HEAT

The New Three-Part Series

Featuring Tyler Monroe

"I once had one in my mouth twice that size," I boast as I adjust the collar of my chef's jacket. "I had it all the way in before it exploded. I swallowed most of it."

"You what?" Drea, the newly hired sous chef stares across the counter at me, a knife at the ready in her hand. "There's no way you did that, Cadence. I don't believe you."

"Whether you believe me or not isn't relevant." I turn back towards my prep station. "I know what I'm capable of and I know that if I was given the chance, I'd happily prove that I could take Tyler Monroe's in one swallow. I'd do it right now if I have the chance."

"You'd think I'd have a say in that, no?"

I stop with my hand in mid-air. No one else is supposed to be in the kitchen right now. The only people in the entire restaurant are the two front-of-the house staff who are busy confirming reservations. They're both also women. That means that there's no way in hell either of them just asked that question considering the voice attached to it is all kinds of deep and sexy. I know that voice. I've never heard it in person but I've heard it whenever he's been on television, which seems to be all the time recently.

"Who are you?" Drea asks because she's not only new, she's naïve. She must also be one of the few people working in the restaurant industry in New York who has never seen a picture of him.

"I'm Tyler." I hear footsteps behind me. "I'm Tyler Monroe and you are?"

"Drea Hernandez," she offers. "You're not actually Tyler Monroe, are you?"

"I'm actually him." He chuckles.

I hear shuffling behind me and then in a way too excited tone, Drea screeches out the words no one working in this kitchen should ask. "Can I get your autograph? I have all of your cookbooks at home, but can you sign my jacket?"

I pick that moment to turn around because I know inevitably I'm going to have to face him. He's one of the reasons I applied for this position after I graduated from culinary school. His career is astounding and his accomplishments are nothing short of impressive. He's only twenty-nine-years-old and he's already the owner and chef at one of the most prestigious restaurants in Manhattan.

"I sign your paycheck." He ignores the offer of the pen that Drea is dangling in front of him. "I assume that whatever you're working on needs your attention."

She purses her lips together in a grimace before she tucks the pen back into her pocket. "I thought you were on a book tour."

"I thought you had work to do," he counters. "I'm here for dinner service tonight. I want everything in order."

I stare at his profile. He's striking. His dark hair is long enough to touch the collar of his jacket. His face is covered in stubble. It's no wonder that women come to the restaurant in the hope that he'll be here. I've lost count of how many of my classmates from culinary school have asked if they can stop by to meet him.

"You and I should talk." He suddenly turns to the side so he's facing me directly. "Come with me."

My breath catches at his words. "I have a lot of work to do."

His tongue darts over his bottom lip before he runs it over the top. It's a thoughtless gesture that shouldn't impact me the way that it does. "That can wait."

I lower the knife in my hand onto the cutting board. I smooth my hands over the front of my chef's jacket before I take a deep breath and silently follow him down a corridor toward a makeshift office that I've seen the restaurant manager use to fire those who don't pull their weight.

"If this is about what you overheard, I can explain that," I say the moment we're through the doorway.

He slides the leather jacket he's wearing from his shoulders revealing his muscular, tattooed arms. I look to the open doorway hoping someone, anyone, will save me from this moment.

"I don't need an explanation." He tilts his head to the side as his eyes rake me from head to toe. His gaze stalls on my name, which is sewn on the front of my jacket in red thread. "I'm going to assume you were talking about one of my signature dishes when you said you could fit the entire thing in your mouth."

I bite my bottom lip when he takes a step closer his eyes riveted to my face.

"That's what you were talking about isn't it, Cadence?"

My lips part slightly as I pull in a deep breath. "No. I was talking about… I was actually talking about your…"

Coming 2016

ABOUT THE AUTHOR

Deborah Bladon has never read a romance hero she didn't like. Her love for romance novels began when she was old enough to board the bus, library card in hand to check out the newest Harlequin paperbacks. She's a Canadian by heart, and by passport, but you can often spot her in New York City sipping a latte and looking for inspiration for her next story. Manhattan is definitely her second home.

She cherishes her family and believes that each day is a gift for writing, for reading, and for loving.

14616995R00155

Printed in Great Britain
by Amazon.co.uk, Ltd.,
Marston Gate.